MY GINGERBREAD EVER AFTER

BY USA TODAY AUTHOR
ERIN BEDFORD

Cover Design by Moonstruck Cover Designs
www.moonstruckcoverdesigns.com

Editing by Makenzie Frazier

ALSO BY ERIN BEDFORD

The Underground Series
Chasing Rabbits
Chasing Cats
Chasing Princes
Chasing Shadows
Chasing Hearts

The Crimes of Alice
The Crimes of Alice
Hatter's Heart

The Mary Wiles Chronicles
Marked by Hell
Bound by Hell
Deceived by Hell
Tempted by Hell
Betrayed by Hell

Fairy Tale Bad Boys
Beauty and the Hunter
Wendy's Pirate
More Precious Than Gold

Starcrossed Dragons
Riding Lightning
Grinding Frost
Swallowing Fire
Pounding Earth

Curse of the Fairy Tales
Rapunzel Untamed
Rapunzel Unveiled

Her Angels
Heaven's Embrace
Heaven's A Beach
Heaven's Most Wanted

The Monsters You Know
Courting Her Monsters

<u>**House of Durand**</u>
Indebted to the Vampires
Wanted by the Vampires
Protected by the Vampires
Embrace of the Vampires
Tempted by the Butler
Loved by the Vampires
Huntress of the Vampires
Judged by the Vampires
Imprisoned by the Vampires

<u>**Academy of Witches**</u>
Witching On A Star
As You Witch
Witch You Were Here
Just Witch It
Summer Witchin'

<u>**Children of the Fallen**</u>
Death In Her Eyes
Fire In Her Blood

<u>**Wicked Crown**</u>
Little Morning Star
When Hell Freezes Over
To Hell With It

<u>**House of Van Helsing**</u>
Her Cross To Bear
Blood Betrayal

The Beast of the Fae Court
Granting Her Wish
Vampire CEO

MY GINGERBREAD EVER AFTER

BY USA TODAY AUTHOR

ERIN BEDFORD

CHAPTER ONE

IT WAS OFFICIAL. I was a shlong candy-making genius!

"Come on, baby," I murmured to the delicate tray, moving at a glacial pace as I lifted the tray from the freezer. I wanted to keep the closest thing to a perfect dick candy in Candipolis. "That's it. Come to mama."

"This is a new low, even for you, Tara."

I shot a glare over my shoulder at the black cat sitting on the kitchen table with a judgmental look on his feline face. "I don't know what you mean."

Ignoring my familiar, Jax, I trudged toward the counter. I could not break this one. I didn't want to start over.

"I mean, that you have extended from talking to a cat to talking to inanimate objects." Jax yawned and laid his head back on his paws.

Snorting, I took another slow step to the counter. "If I didn't talk to you, then you would just get pissy and I'd find hairballs in my favorite shoes."

"I did that one time! And that's because —"

The shop door burst open. I jolted, and the cast slipped from my hands. When it cracked, I let out a cry of despair. So many hours. So much work. Wasted.

"Uh — hello? Is anyone here?" Someone called from the front of the shop.

I stared down at my latest creation and sighed. I stepped over it and walked through the kitchen to the swinging door. The place looked different from when my grandma owned the cottage. I'd added a front shop to the main part of the gingerbread house, expanding the back into a formal bedroom. Sleeping by the kitchen stove might have been good enough for my grandma, but I needed my privacy and a soft mattress.

I picked up some stray candy off the counter. A pretty blonde-haired woman stood on the other side of me, her eyes blinking rapidly. "What can I do for you?"

The blonde-haired woman's almond-colored eyes scanned the surrounding shelves, taking in the glass containers of candies and suckers, chocolates, and chewing gums. I worked hard to make the place look like a candy land.

When she didn't answer my question, I cleared my throat until she brought her eyes back to me. They slid over my face, no doubt taking in my freckled face and larger-than-life curly brown hair I'd tied up on my head, before moving on to the black dress with hot pink tights and underskirt. I didn't exactly scream witch or candy maker, but something in between.

"Uh..." she started, the displeasure at what she was seeing clear on her face. "Am I in the right place?"

I tapped the counter with my long black and green striped nails. "I don't know, are you?"

Glancing behind her quickly as if someone was watching her. Of course, no one was there. The shop deserted at nine at night. No one wanted to come this late.

I'd probably get better sales if I moved my shop closer to the village, but this was my grandma's house. Call me sentimental, but I didn't want to change it more than I already had.

Leaning forward, she lowered her voice, her cupid bow lips pursed. "Are you the... you know... the witch?"

My lips ticked up at one side. I leaned forward on the counter until I was eye-to-eye with her. "That depends... are you a hunter?"

I highly doubted it by the fancy silk gown covering her body or the dainty gloves on her hands. However, I had to ask. Gotta be careful, witches weren't exactly everyone's favorite magical beings. Not since grandma's little... incident.

The woman blinked at me, straightening at once. "No!"

"Alright." I straightened as well, adjusting the apron strings around my waist. "What can I do for you?"

She licked her lips and whispered so low I couldn't quite catch it.

"Sorry, I didn't catch that?"

"A curse!" she squeaked out and then pinched her lips together, her eyes wide with panic.

I let out a little chuckle.

Humans. So guilty about every want and desire. Every need for justice and retribution. They always wanted us supernaturals to do their dirty work for them. Then they had someone to blame when it all went wrong.

"Okay, a curse." I nodded and moved to the back counter, reaching out to pick out a few items I'd need to make what she wanted. "What kind of curse?"

"Why does that matter?" The quiver in her voice made me pause for a moment.

I turned back to her, my brow arched, "Are you sure you want to do this?"

She stared at me for a long moment before dropping her eyes to the counter. She took a deep breath, as if steeling herself. Then her eyes flicked back up to mine, a hard resolve in them. "Yes. I'm sure. He must pay."

He?

Hmmm.

Jilted lover, perhaps?

"Alright, is there a specific type of curse you want?" I turned back to my shelves, scooping a few beads of sorrow into the felt bag. "Boils? Flatulence?" I smirked over my shoulder. "Impotence?"

She wrung her hands in front of her. "Do I have to decide now?"

Shifting from the counter, the felt bag in my hands, I cocked my head to the side. "You want to think about it, good woman. You should never be too quick to punish. Then it's over too quickly." I shared a grin with her before bringing the bag over to her.

I waved my hand over the contents of the bag, muttering a few incantations. The contents glowed bright blue before settling into the bag. "Here." I held the bag out to her. "Get the bastard to ingest some of this. In his drink. In food. Anything. But make sure your intentions are clear when you do it."

"What do you mean?" she frowned, not taking the bag from me.

"Think really hard about what you want to happen while you add the mixture to his food or drink and it will happen."

"How long does it take to work?" She reached for the bag.

I pulled it back from her before she could take it.

"Within twenty-four hours." I paused and held out my other hand. "I'm not running a charity."

"Oh, yeah." She pulled out a small bag and dropped it into my hand.

I weighed it in my hand for a moment, then peeked inside. Shiny gold coins glinted back at me. Satisfied with the amount, I released the bag into her hand and smiled. "Pleasure doing business with you."

The woman gave me a weak smile back. "Thank you."

I poured the coins on the counters and started counting them out. When the door didn't close, I glanced up. The woman stood there in the middle of the shop.

I paused mid-count. "Did you need something else?"

Chewing on her lower lip, the woman turned to me. "What if something goes wrong? What should I do? I don't want to... you know... kill him."

"Pfft," I waved her off. "Don't worry about it. You can't kill anyone with that curse. And if you run into any issues, just let me know."

"Really?" A sparkle filled her eyes.

I gave her my best customer service smile, though I had a sinking feeling in my stomach. "Absolutely."

When she was gone, I sagged and scooped the coins back into the bag before putting them in the pocket of my apron. Walking to the shop door, I pulled the curtains and locked the door, flicking the front light off.

"Do you think that was wise?" Jax popped up on a nearby shelf.

I jumped, a hand on my heart. "Candy fucker, Jax. Don't do that." I walked around the shelf. "I don't know what you're talking about. It's just a harmless curse. And that woman is so docile, she's harmless. What's the worst she could do?"

Jax sniffed. "It's the quiet ones you have to watch out for."

CHAPTER TWO

I STARED DOWN AT the newly made creation, my mouth twisted to one side. It took me all week to make this one, and I wasn't going to ruin it for some little revenge plot. Though the coin did help with buying new ingredients.

"In what world is that a dick?" Jax licked his paws and eyed my creation.

Arms crossed, I glared down at the feline. "What would you know about it?"

Jax lowered his paw and eyed me. "I may be a cat, but I know what a human cock looks like and that is not it." He jerked his head toward the candy dick.

I hated to admit it — he was right. The shaft wasn't linear. The mushroom wasn't quite right and the balls... sigh... don't get me started on those.

I pulled my lower lip in between my teeth. "It would be a lot easier to get the shape right with a real one."

The door of the shop slammed open, and a voice yelled out, "Where the fuck are you, witch?"

Shooting a warning look at Jax, I wiped my hands on a nearby towel before heading to the front. I ducked my head out the swinging door and put on a pleasant smile. Sugary sweet. Sugary sweet. You catch more kids with sugar than with... well, I probably shouldn't be taking advice from my grandma right now.

"Hi, can I help you?" My eyes scanned the shop until they landed on a cloaked figure. Almost two heads taller than me, the figure jerked away from one of the nearby shelves full of a variety of bear-shaped gummy candies.

The figure grabbed a long thick one — one of my many failures to make a perfect dick candy — and waved it at me like a sword. "Is this what you call a livelihood, witch? Making trite sweets and cursing unsuspecting men?" His deep voice had a bit of a husky touch to it that would have been attractive had they not been yelling at me.

I cocked my head to the side and blinked at him. "I don't know if I would call it my livelihood. It doesn't make the big coins but I do alright. Of course, I would do better if I weren't so far from the village. However, I think it's important to remember where you came from and my grandma built this cottage. She'd be so upset if I moved it."

"Enough!" The hooded figure shoved the side of one of the shelves and sent it careening into another one until it was a domino effect of shelves.

My hands shot up, and my magic pulsed out, freezing the shelves in place. I glowered at the stranger before pushing the shelves back into place. Each candy that lay smashed on the floor was like a sharp stab of glass in my heart.

"The witch reveals herself at last!"

"You better have the coin to pay for those." I hopped up on the counter and crossed one leg over the other and clicked my tongue. "Now how about you tell us who you are and then we can go from there."

The figure stalked forward, throwing the hood of the cloak off. "You do not recognize your crown prince? You should kneel before me, you bottom feeding swine."

I arched my brow. "Eloquent."

My eyes slid over the revealed face. Gingerbread-colored skin covered an elegant face that looked like it should belong on one of those naked statues everyone raved about.

Black hair, so dark that blue highlights glinted off it in the light, curled at the nape of his neck. The same black speckled his chin and jaw, giving him a dashing sort of look. Or it would have if he didn't have a nasty sneer on those kissable lips. His hateful eyes, the color of the rolling waves on a clear day, narrowed on me.

So, this was the crown prince.

Huh.

I'd expected something else. Someone more pretty. Less melt in your panties... not my panties, of course, someone else's, like those simpering ladies in court.

I tended to keep to myself and stay far away from the large crowds of events. Especially ones that the royalty would frequent. If the townspeople didn't care for witches, the royals definitely couldn't stand us. Hence the grumpy mcgrumpikins before me.

"Do not test me, vile beast." He shook the gummy dick at my face and I couldn't help but smile. He scowled and threw the gummy dick away. My eyes watched it bounce off the floor, which was enough time for the prince to be on me. His hand wrapped around my throat; he shoved me down onto the counter. "I will snap your neck like a twig and no one will mourn your loss."

His body pressed against mine, the hard planes of his form would have been pleasant had he not been threatening me. Something stiff poked me in the leg. Sword? I shifted my knee, and it bobbed. My eyes widened. Not a sword.

Licking my lips, I turned my gaze back to the prince. "You could do that. But then you wouldn't get what you came here for. You want to tell me what you want?"

The prince glowered at me for a moment longer, his hand pulsating around my neck as if he were contemplating killing me anyway before he released me with a shove.

I cautiously sat up, rubbing my throat with one hand. That was going to bruise. "Why don't we start over?"

Jaw tightening, the prince jerked his head once.

Taking that as a yes, I hopped off the counter and stepped up to him. "I'm Tara."

Staring down at me as if I was a bug beneath his shoe, he reluctantly bit out, "William."

Of course it was.

"Well, William."

"That's your highness to you, demon whore."

"Whoa, whoa." I held my hands up and stepped back. "What's up with all the name-calling? You don't see me coming into your house, attacking you, breaking your stuff, and calling you names. And I'll have you know I've never even met a devil or demon. We don't exactly run in the same circles."

"It doesn't matter. You're wicked, just like the rest of them." He closed in on me until my legs kicked the counter. "And I will kill you for what you did to me."

"What I did to you?" I glanced over at him, taking a moment longer than I should have to take in the broad chest that was peppered with black hair, a few of the buttons of his shirt undone. "I've never even met you. Why would I want to do anything to you?" I didn't mention the fact that I was itching to curse him now for his attitude and general unpleasantness.

"Why don't you tell me? You're the one who cursed me." His breath was hot on my face and smelled of cinnamon sticks.

I sighed and shook my head. "We can keep going round and round about this all night and not get anywhere. Why don't you start at the beginning? Why do you think you're cursed?"

Prince William stepped back and jerked his cloak from his shoulders. It fluttered to the ground, revealing his crimson-colored silk shirt and deep brown trousers. My gaze lingered on the front of his pants where a prominent tent protruded from him. "This is why I am cursed!"

Trying not to think about how massive a cock the prince must have to make such a big tent, I jerked my eyes back up to his unamused ones. "I think that's more of a doctor's problem, not a witch's problem. Have you been taking any of those performance-enhancement drugs?"

He grabbed his cock in his large hand and growled, "I don't need any help in that department."

"So, you want me to do what? Help you get it down?" I jerked a hand at his impressive erection. "That's not really my department."

"Then maybe this is..." He jerked the ties of his pants and shoved his pants down.

Automatically, I shoved my eyes to the ceiling of the shop. What had I done to deserve this? Am I paying for my grandma's immoral behavior? She wasn't always crazy. It wasn't until the end that she started eating kids. But I wasn't anything like her. So, why was I getting the short end of the... well... dick as it was?

"Oh, now you're shy?" The prince huffed a disbelieving laugh. "You can curse my dick, but you can't look at it? How is that fair?"

I licked my lips and slowly lowered my gaze from the ceiling to meet his gaze. "As I said, I didn't curse you or your dick. So don't get all pissy at me."

"You would be pissy too if your dick looked like this." He gestured down at his lower half, and against my will, my eyes followed his movements.

It took me a moment to realize what I was looking at. When my brain finally caught up to what was in front of me, a laugh charged up my throat.

"Your dick is a... is a..." I couldn't quite get the words out, a laugh tickling in my throat. I covered my mouth, trying to shove it back down where it belonged.

"Yes," William gritted out with a snarl, "My dick is a candy cane."

CHAPTER THREE

THE MAN MIGHT BE an alpha asshole, but he had the most beautiful penis I'd ever seen in my life. It had girth, length, and a perfectly shaped mushroom top. If not for the white and red striped color of his flesh, I'd be on my knees before him right then and there.

"You can stop staring now," the prince snarled, jerking his cock back into his pants and buttoning them closed. Though it was pointless. His cock jabbed against the front of his pants, leaving a permanent erection visible.

I lowered my hand slowly, trying my best not to burst out laughing again. "Um... so..." I coughed and turned my eyes to the side. "You're saying I cursed you with this?"

"No shit. I didn't just one day wake up and decide 'I know what would make my cock better, a candy cane coating'!" He took an aggressive step toward me.

I held my hands up to ward him off. "Hey, don't come at me. I didn't curse you. I've never even met you before. We don't exactly hang out in the same circles," I ended dryly.

"Then you sold the curse to someone to use it on me and you are going to fix it." He moved toward me until his chest pressed against my hands.

"No way, your highness." I reached behind my counter and pulled out a framed picture I kept for just this occasion. "Read it and suck it."

William snatched the picture from my hands and read under his breath, "Here at the Gingerbread House we are not liable or responsible for any and all curses/spells obtained for personal or professional use. Any resulting actions are the responsibility of the caster and/or wisher and are not a direct reflection of the witch in question."

He glanced up from the frame, his eyes narrowed. "So, you just sell curses to anyone without finding out what they planned to do with it? How is that a safe business practice?"

I threw my hands up and rolled my eyes. "Look, I don't have time to be interrogating every single customer that walks through my door. And besides, there are contingencies."

"Contingencies? Like what?" He braced his hands on the counter, blocking me in.

I swallowed, trying to ignore the thing poking me in the stomach. "Like they can't wish to kill anyone or maim them permanently."

Leaning into me until our noses almost touched, the prince growled, "That leaves a lot of wiggle room for someone to curse my cock into a fucking candy cane!"

Tired of going round and round with the man, I flicked my fingers, shoving him a few feet back. "Look, I can't control what people do with the curses they purchase. Do you have any idea who could have cursed you?" Though, based on the prince's personality, I had a feeling the list was quite long.

Eyes wide at the show of my magic, the prince kept a wary distance from me. "I'm the prince. There are quite a lot of people who would want to harm me."

I arched my brow. "Well, cursing your cock sounds like something personal. You don't have any scorned lovers—" I cut myself off, something tickling at the back of my head.

William dragged his fingers through his hair and shook his head. "I have many lovers... is it my fault if they believe a one-night stand is something more?"

Jax jumped up on the counter and licked his paw. "I bet that woman who came here earlier this week was the one who did it."

The prince eyeballed my familiar before looking at me. "What woman?"

I shrugged my shoulders. "Pretty, rich, blonde. I'm not sure that narrows it down much for you." I tossed over my shoulder as I walked toward the back. "Look, I can't help you if I don't know the exact parameters of the curse."

The prince stomped after me, slamming the swinging door against the wall. The items on the wall shook and a jar of sugar fell off the shelf. I barely caught it with my magic before it smashed to the ground.

"Would you calm the fuck down?" I sighed and dug through a drawer, searching for my reversal spells.

He slammed his hands down on the kitchen counter. "If your favorite body part was increasingly becoming a candy cane, you'd have a little trouble controlling your emotions as well."

I glanced up from the drawer. "So, it wasn't all at once?"

His lips twisted to the side. "No. It seems the bitch decided I had to suffer even further. It spread a little more every time I had sex with someone. At first, it was amusing. The ladies liked it too…" his lips curled up into a smirk. "It doesn't just look like a candy cane; it tastes like one."

The heated look in his eyes made something low in me tighten deliciously. "Is that so?" I paused for a moment and then turned to him. "So, you're saying that your penis started changing into a candy cane every time you had sex with someone and you kept doing it?"

William didn't even have the good sense to look guilty or ashamed of it.

"How many times did you do it to get it like that?" I jerked a hand at his crotch.

He adjusted his pants and shrugged. "What can I say? I like sex."

"Now, I am starting to see why she cursed you," I muttered to myself under my breath. To the prince, I said, "And at what point did you decide it was a good idea to figure out what the hell was going on?"

"When, after my fun, it wouldn't go down." He gestured at the tent in his pants with a sneer. "I can't lead a strategy meeting or train the troops with a raging hard on. No one would take me seriously."

I snorted. "As if they did before."

A low rumble came from his chest. "Remember who you are talking to, witch. I can have you thrown in the dungeon for your part in this. However, I would call us even if you can just fix it."

Blowing out a hard breath that fluttered my bangs, I walked over to the prince. "Look. I will try my best to fix your penis."

"Good, then get to it." he snapped his finger at me.

"For the sake of saving time, I'm going to ignore that." I gave him a warning look. "But unfortunately, I don't have the supplies to work on it and the trip to get the items isn't something I want to take alone, let alone at a time like this..." I gestured to the darkening sky outside the window.

"If safety is an issue, I will escort you." He palmed the hilt of his sword. "You will be safe from harm and everyone will get what they want."

I eyeballed him. "How am I getting anything out of this? As far as I can see, I'm the one who is doing all the work, for free, might I add, when I have no legal responsibility to help you."

The prince gave me a long look before scowling. "Fine. What would you like? Coin? Favors? A recommendation to move to a shop in town?"

I started to say the last one, then my eyes caught on the mold of the dick I'd been working on and an idea came to me. Crossing my arms over my chest, I saddled up to the prince. "I want your penis."

The surprise on the prince's face was almost worth it until his eyes skimmed over my body, lingering on my boobs. "Well, I don't usually dip my cock into such lower beings, but I suppose I could make an except—"

"What?" My eyes widened and then I jerked back, waving my hands in front of me. "Ew. No. I wouldn't touch you with a ten-foot pole."

The prince gaped at me with disbelief. Apparently, he wasn't used to women telling him no.

I moved over to the counter and held up my candy mold. "I am trying to make the perfect candy dick and seem to be coming up short. And I happened to notice that your penis is not completely unpleasant to look at and would be perfect for my mold. Plus," I smiled coyly, "I'd sell a ton to the ladies of the village who could have their very own royal cock to suck on."

William eyeballed the mold for a long moment before jerking his head once in agreement. "Very well. I can agree with that. Let's go."

I lifted a hand at the window. "But... it's... it's... we won't be able to get there and back before it gets dark..."

Turning toward the front door, the prince smiled. "What? Is the great witch afraid of the dark?"

My eyes narrowed into slits and I grumbled, "Let me grab my bag and coat."

I ducked into the closet, Jax rubbing against my legs.

"Do you think this is a wise choice?" he purred out. "You know who comes out at night and you'll have to pass right by his house on the way to your aunt's place."

I grit my teeth and bit out, "It will be fine. I'm sure he won't even notice I'm there."

"Famous last words." Jax yowled. "Don't say I didn't warn you."

CHAPTER FOUR

JAX CHASED ME OUT of the closet and into the main shop where Prince Candy Cane Dick waited. "I still don't think this is a good idea. You know he won't just let you walk by his home without getting his fix." We stepped outside and I locked the store behind me, throwing up a protection spell to keep out unwanted thieves and miscreants.

"Who?" the prince asked once he was standing next to his horse.

"No one," I bit out between clenched teeth. To Jax, I said, "You could come with me and make sure that doesn't happen..."

Jax sniffed, lifting his nose in the air. "No, thank you. You know he doesn't like me."

I coughed, shooting him a warning look.

"What am I missing?" William asked, petting his horse with a suspicious frown.

I skipped to him and grinned, patting him on the side of the face, "Nothing at all Willie. Let's go."

"Do not call me that." William stalked after me with a growl. "You have no respect for your betters."

I smirked over my shoulder. "When you see one, let me know."

"Where is your horse?" he asked before I could get more than a few feet away. "Do you intend to walk the entire way?"

I snorted. "Not everyone has the money to own and maintain a horse, your highness." I spun on my heel, walking backward as we talked. "What, is the prince too good to walk in the forest? Are you afraid of getting your precious boots dirty?" I clucked my tongue at his shoes and wrinkled my nose.

I probably shouldn't have been poking the bear. The prince was just so easy to rile up. Since I was going to be stuck with the grumpy prince for an unknown amount of time, I wanted to at least get some amusement out of it.

"I am not worried about messing up my boots." he glanced around my home and scowled. "You don't exactly have anywhere for me to leave her until we get back."

Pausing, I tapped my chin with my finger. It would be faster if we didn't have to drag his horse along with us. Plus, there were quite a few creatures in the woods that would love to chow down on the horse, and I didn't want to attract their attention.

Not seeing another way out of it, I waved my hand at the horse and muttered a few enchantments. The horse stopped moving, freezing up in place, one leg up as if it were about to step forward, its hair fluttering slightly in the breeze.

"What the hell?" the prince jerked the reins, glaring at me when the horse didn't move. "What did you do? Undo it."

I shook my head. "She's fine. I just did a stasis spell. She's still alive and will be perfectly fine until we get back."

William surveyed his horse for a long moment, before scowling. "Fine. But if this does anything to harm her afterward, you will pay."

I waved my hand at him and started forward again. "Yeah. Yeah. I know. I'll pay.

You'll kill me. Whatever. Come on, we are losing daylight."

The sun played on along the edges of the horizon as I strode into the forest edge. The trees encompassed us, wrapping us up in their dark shadows until the sun barely flitted through the canopy. I wrapped my cloak around myself, hugging it tighter, as if that was enough to hide my scent from the creatures of the forest.

A warm presence crept up beside me. I glanced over to see the prince keeping pace with me. His eyes searched the shadows, his shoulders bunched and his jaw tight. It seemed I didn't need to warn him about the dangers of the forest. At least I didn't have to worry about keeping both of us safe.

"What are we looking for anyway?" the prince asked after we walked along the worn dirt pathway through the forest. "A magic gold cup? A unicorn's horn?"

I cocked a brow at him. "You've read too many fairy tales. We're going to my aunt's first. She has something I need."

"What? A heart? Because yours is as icy as your cunt must be," he replied dryly, adjusting his cock in his pants.

"Haha, if any of us have an icy heart, it's you. You're the one fucking through the kingdom like your dick is going out of style." I giggled and flicked my puffy, dark hair over my shoulder. "For all I know, it probably is."

"I don't fuck everyone. I haven't fucked you," he pointed out with a sneer.

I opened my mouth to retort. Something made me pause.

My head turned to the side, listening.

Something was hunting us.

"Sorry," I continued to talk as if it weren't watching us. "I don't let men with the personality of a rabid possum near my vagina. For all I know, you caught something in your... travels." I trailed off with a coy smile.

"Very funny. I'll have you know I have a charm for that."

"I'm sure you do." I swung my arms by my side, acting as if I had all the time in the world to get to where I needed to go. The birds shrieked and flew away in a hurry. It was getting close now.

The prince paused; his head turned to the side as if he too sensed something was wrong.

"So, what did you do to piss this woman off, anyway?" I began, trying to fill the silence. "You can't be that good of a fuck."

William's gaze slid over to my face with a smug sense of pride.

"Really?" I arched my brow and then shook my head. "I'm surprised you can get into anyone's skirts with that winning personality."

"I will have you know, most women find me charming."

"Yeah, insane ones," I muttered under my breath and then threw an arm out, stopping the prince in his tracks. "Wait."

"What is it?" the prince pressed against my arm, his eyes wide.

"Shhh," I told him, letting my senses reach out around me. The auras of several small animals skittered underneath the brush, none of them a concern to me. An owl fluttered a couple of trees away. There was something else... something prowling in a circle around us, its aura a deep red full of hunger and malevolent intentions.

The metal of the prince's sword unsheathing zinged through the air and was exactly enough to send the beast into a head-on charge for us.

"Men." I sighed and flipped around to face the beast.

William followed suit, holding his sword out in front of him like that was going to protect us against this creature.

Its shape was large, almost eight feet, standing on its hind legs. Luckily, it was much shorter when on all fours, as its long black claws dug into the ground while it pounded toward us. Its dark eyes burned a molten red as it flicked between me and the prince. Its snout huffed a growl before the mouth curled back, baring sharp teeth.

"Stand back, witch. I will slay this monster." The prince shoved me aside and put himself right in the pathway of the so-called monster.

I caught myself on a nearby tree and watched as the prince braced himself for an attack. For half a second, I thought maybe he'd actually kill the beast. Then his sword smashed against the razor-sharp claws and the blade broke clean in half.

Pity.

Pushing away from the tree, I held my hands out and called to the prince, "Alright, your highness, why don't you get back and let me take care of this?"

The prince stumbled back from the creature to give me a disbelieving look. "What are you talking about? Don't be stupid. Stay back, witch!"

Huffing a breath in annoyance, I twisted my wrist as I wrote my spell, "Why do men always think we need saving? Can't we be just as badass as you? I mean, really?" I pushed my magic out and wrapped it around the creature's legs and pulled it tight.

The creature roared as it collapsed on the ground, trying and failing to claw at my magical ropes. I continued to wrap the rope around the creature until its arms were bound and a noose tightened around its neck.

Holding the loose length of the rope tight, I peered down at the creature with a scowl. "You're being ridiculous."

The creature gave me a growling huff, jerking his head toward the prince. Or more pointedly, at his crotch.

I lifted my eyes to the sky. "That's not because of me. He's cursed."

The creature blew out a hot breath as if to say, yeah right.

Over my shoulder, I called out to the prince, "Hey drop your pants."

"What?" the prince still had the hilt of his broken sword in his hand. His face slackened at either my abilities or my request.

Jerking the rope a bit tighter, I licked my lips. "Show him your dick, William."

"Uh, no. I don't think so."

I understood the caution in his voice, probably thinking the creature was going to bite it off or something. The longer he put it off, the more irritated the creature was going to get and I couldn't hold him forever. I was good, but not that good.

"Just do it." I eyeballed him firmly. "Trust me."

Reluctantly, and I mean, with extreme resistance, the prince dropped his sword and untied his pants, dropping them to the ground.

The creature gave one look at the prince's dick and coughed a growling laugh before starting to shrink. Fur receded and a naked man lay in the creature's spot. The ropes shrunk with him until it looked like I was about to have fabulously kinky sex with the lean man.

"I'm guessing you know this man?" the prince pulled his pants back on and inched toward us.

The naked man flicked his messy brown hair and smiled a razor-sharp grin at the prince. "I'm Percy, Tara's mate."

CHAPTER FIVE

I YANKED ON THE rope until Percy let out a grunt. "I am not your mate. Stop telling people that."

Percy simply flashed those sharp teeth at me, the whole row of them white enough to blind a person. "I would be if you'd stop playing hard to get."

I rolled my eyes and glanced over at the prince. "What is it with you men? Every time we say no, you think we mean yes. Sometimes no is actually no. Not an, I-want-you-to-convince-me, no. Or, we-need-a-safe-word, kind of no. When I say no, I mean fuck off and leave me alone or I'll turn your dick into something worse than what his is!"

Percy pouted up at me, his big brown eyes doing that shiny puppy dog thing, until I let out an aggravated groan and released the spell with a huff. The rope disappeared and Percy climbed to his feet, showing that he, too, was happy to see me.

Turning my back on the shifter, I walked back over to the prince. "Come on. I want to get to my aunt's before she goes to bed."

"Your Aunt Nutmeg?" Percy asked, chasing after us while putting his clothes on.

"Not that it's any of your business, but yes," I threw over my shoulder and stalked forward.

The prince followed me with a frown marring his face. I was sure he had questions. I didn't want to answer them right now or ever, really.

"Well then, you're going the wrong way," Percy stated as he caught up with us.

"No, I'm not." Why was he following us again? Oh right. He doesn't know when to take no for an answer. "I think I know where my aunt lives. She's lived there for the last hundred and four years."

"A hundred and four?" the prince finally piped in. "How long do you witches live?"

I smirked at him. "Wouldn't you like to know?"

Percy interrupted us, shoving between the prince and me. "But she lives by the Milky Way River off the Chocolate Frosting Bay now."

I halted, my hands on my hips. "No, she doesn't. She lives on the icy peak of Vanilla Mountain. She always has."

Percy shook his head. "Nope. Not since last week when she threw out her hip trying to get up the mountain. The squirrels helped her move and made quite a racket doing it."

I pursed my lips. "Why would she move without telling me?"

Shrugging, Percy adjusted the velvet green vest over his bare chest. "Maybe she didn't want to worry you. But in any case, at least you don't have to see that wretched bitch Viola." He shuddered as if he had tasted something bad.

I shoved a finger at his muscular chest. "Hey, that wretched bitch is my best friend and another stop on our trip, so you better shut up and be nice if you want to keep your ability to speak."

William watched our interaction with a curious gaze.

"Fine, fine." Percy held his hands up in front of him before turning his attention to the prince. "So... candy cane dick, huh? She cursed you?" He pointed his thumb at me.

"No," I snapped, punching him in the arm with a sneer. "People need to stop assuming that."

"Well, you do own a candy shop and sell curses..." Percy trailed off his hands in his pockets and shrugged. "It's kind of hard not to connect the dots."

"See," William nodded smugly. "I'm not the only one."

"Just because I sold the curse doesn't mean I came up with it. I do have to give your girl points for her creativity." I grinned sweetly. "Besides, you're the one who kept fucking around until it looked like that. A sane person would have stopped and got it looked at before it became this worrisome. It would have been easy to fix then. But nooooo, you had to get your dick wet until it became a problem. Then you wanted my help. Pfft."

Typical.

"You're one to talk. You're more obsessed with getting dick than anyone I know. Or else you wouldn't be trying to make a candy mold of it," William pointed out with a raise of his brow.

"A candy mold?" Percy looked between the two of us before settling on me. "Why didn't you say so? I would have happily given you the shape of my dick for your use."

I gave the prince a look that said thanks a lot before answering Percy, "Because I don't want your dick anywhere near me or my candy."

The prince tsked.

Frowning at his back, I couldn't help but ask, "What?"

He shook his head, not stopping his trek. "It's no wonder you're so tightly wound. You won't take the dick freely offered to you."

I gaped at him. "Excuse me, if I have standards—" I shot a look at Percy, "no offense meant," before using my magic to shove the prince forward a few steps. He tripped on his feet and fell face-first into a chocolate pit. I covered my mouth with my hand, hiding the grin on my face.

The prince jerked up from the pit, his face covered with dark sludge running down the front of his shirt and pants. He saw me laughing and growled.

I wasn't fast enough to dodge the ball of chocolate that pelted me right in the face.

"Ah!" I cried out, swiping the thick brown muck off my face. Licking my fingers, I glared at the prince. "You're going to pay for that." I flicked a finger, and the prince found himself flat on his back in the chocolate.

"Is that it?" the prince jeered. "You're too afraid to face me head on, so you use your magic?"

"Not afraid." I cocked my head to the side. "Lazy. There's a difference and besides... that's a good look on you. Maybe you wouldn't have your little issue if you looked like that."

Percy watched from the sidelines with a bemused expression.

"My issue is with psycho women taking things too far, not my looks," William practically shouted, his erection even more prominent with the chocolate coating the front of his pants.

A dirty voice in my head wondered what his dick tasted like as a chocolate-covered candy cane.

"Ugh, great. Now I'm going to attract all kinds of bugs and wildlife. Thank you so much, witch bitch." The sarcasm hung heavy in his words, and it made the next decision even easier.

"There's a river just a bit further. You can clean up there."

The prince glanced toward the pathway before giving me a final glare and stomping in that direction, leaving Percy and me behind.

"I don't get it."

"What?" I asked the shifter, a small smile lingering on my lips.

"Why didn't you just clean him with your magic?" Percy cocked his head at me. "I know you can. I've seen you do it."

I swiped the chocolate off my face with a magic hand, letting it fall to the ground. "So? Doesn't mean I have to use my powers on that arrogant ass."

"I think you like him."

A snort-laugh escaped me. "What? Don't be ridiculous. He's a pompous ass who got cursed because he kept fucking around on the women he bedded."

Percy shrugged. "I'm just saying. Maybe you just want to see him naked, is all. I wouldn't fault you. Did you see his equipment? I can't compete with that."

I rolled my eyes. "Part of that is the spell. I highly doubt he's that hung. And anyway, I don't get wet over a nasty personality."

"Oh, really?" Percy saddled up to my side, brushing a clawed finger along my cheek. "So, what does get you wet?"

I gave him a flat look before walking away without a word. Then I flicked a finger and hit Percy with a face full of chocolate mud.

"Motherfucking bitchface!"

I grinned to myself as I walked around the bend and came face to face with a sight that made my panties turn nonexistent.

CHAPTER SIX

AS I ROUNDED THE corner and came face to face with a bare chested prince, I realized maybe Percy had a point.

Eyes glued to the sight before me, my feet wouldn't move any further. Milky colored water dripped down his chest, sliding across the hard ridges of his abs and dipping into the top of his pants. I licked my lips. The sudden urge to get down on my knees and lick every inch of that milky water off his... well... everything.

When my eyes slid up to his face, I jolted. William was staring right at me, a heated look in his eyes and a smirk on his lips. That smirk killed the sexy trance.

I stalked down the path, keeping my eyes firmly above his shoulders. "Are you about done? We need to get moving. I don't want to spend the night in the woods."

"Almost, just a few more places to clean." The prince slid his hand over his throat and down his chest. My eyes — the traitorous bastards — followed the movement until it stopped at the edge of his pants.

He huffed a laugh. "You are not as unmoved by me as you think."

My gaze flicked back up to his face and narrowed. "I'm not blind. Don't think it's anything to do with you."

I stopped by the edge of the milky river; the water splashed slightly up on the shore. "Where's your shirt?"

The prince jerked his head near a rock where his shirt laid out practically transparent from being washed. I could dry it off with my magic or let him walk around bare chested for a while until it dried on its own. It was a hard choice. One that made my thighs slicker by the minute.

In the end, I picked his shirt up and shook it out. The material dried instantly. I handed the shirt to William. "Here."

Jaw tight and his eyes hard, William reached for his shirt. "If you could have done that, why didn't you in the first place?"

I shrugged. "Amusement."

Turning away from the prince while he dressed, I pretended to be interested in the candy cane coloring of my nails. Maybe I should change them. With the prince's condition, it seemed a bit overkill to have them that color right now. I shook my hands, and the color changed to deep red. I frowned. No. I shook my hands again. They changed to a blue-green, the color of the prince's eyes. Couldn't have that.

"What are you doing?"

I jumped, letting out a little eep. I spun around and bumped into the prince's chest. "What the hell? Why are you so close to me?"

The prince just did that stupid smirk of his before jerking his head at my hands. "If you can do magic so easily, why do you need an escort? You didn't look like you needed a protector when fighting that shifter. Where did he go?" His cyan gaze scanned the trees behind me.

I clucked my tongue and pushed back from him. I needed some breathing space before I jumped that candy cane dick.

"Percy is around somewhere. He'll pop up, eventually." I then muttered to myself, "In my experience, when you least expect it."

"Who is he to you, anyway?" He tucked his shirt into his pants, my eyes flicking down to the bulge in his pants.

"More importantly," I sidestepped the prince and stepped over to the river's edge. "How do you clean your dick when it's a candy cane? Doesn't water dissolve that kind of candy?"

The prince stayed quiet.

Pivoting, I eyeballed him suspiciously. "You have been cleaning it, haven't you?"

He avoided eye contact.

My nose crinkled up, my lips twisting to the side. "That's... ugh... so gross."

William scowled. "You wouldn't be judging if it was your parts that could disintegrate in the shower."

"I can't believe you had sex with all those women and haven't cleaned your dick in between!" I stepped away from him, all of my attraction to him evaporating into thin air.

"Don't be ridiculous." The prince growled and gestured at his crotch. "I didn't stop cleaning it until the candy cane curse fully covered it and by then I stopped having sex. What kind of man do you think I am?"

I eyeballed his crotch and smirked, "Apparently, the kind who hasn't cleaned his dick in days."

Pressing his lips together tightly, William jerked the ties of his pants and the next thing I knew, I was staring at the massive candy cane once more.

I gulped.

Not dropping eye contact, he knelt by the river and scooped up handfuls of milky water. Wrapping his fingers around his cock, he smoothed the water up and down his length. I tried not to watch. I really did. I fought against the urge to look down as long as I could until I found them dipping down and locking onto the movements of his hand.

He wasn't even pretending to clean himself now and stroked himself at a quickening pace, pulling over the tip and down to cup his red and white striped balls, squeezing and pulling them lightly before grabbing hold of his cock again.

"Are you almost done?" I croaked out, licking my lips. My eyes sneaked up to meet his ardent gaze.

He let out a growling grunt. "Almost done."

I should make him stop. He was plenty clean now. There was no reason for him to continue. Except I couldn't. I couldn't stop him even if the king himself was standing there with us.

His hand moved faster now, his large fingers barely touching around his thick cock, the tip glistening as he got closer to his release.

For a moment, I imagined what he would do if I knelt before him. If I took that candy cane striped cock in my hands and wrapped my lips around the tip of the mushroom top. I didn't have much of a gag reflex, but even I was skeptical, as well as turned on, that I wouldn't be able to take all of him.

I licked my lips once more. I could almost taste him now. Would he taste like candy cane or his own natural flavor? I hated to admit that I wanted to know more than anything at that moment.

He came a moment later, the white and red creamy substance spurted out over his hand like a melted candy cane. He pumped himself a few more times, getting it all out before releasing his cock.

Lifting his hand up, he slid his tongue out and licked his palm, never breaking eye contact with me.

"Uh... so does it really taste like it looks?" I winced at the husky sound of my voice.

The prince smirked. "Why don't you come find out?"

More than half tempted, I stepped forward and then shook my head, putting my hands behind my back before I did something I regretted. I cleared my throat and shifted my gaze to anywhere else but him. "If you're quite done, then can we get moving? I'd like to sleep in a bed tonight and not on the forest floor."

William chuckled, and water splashed.

I snuck a look at him, half relieved and half disappointed that he had put his dick back in his pants. I wish he would put away that smug look on his face. If he kept looking at me like that, I was going to do more than curse him.

"Let's go already, your highness." I crossed my arms over my chest and sauntered down the pathway toward the dark chocolate coated bridge that arched over the milky river. So far, we have run into a few hiccups. Nothing I couldn't handle. I just hoped that my luck held up, and we didn't encounter anything out of the scope of my abilities.

CHAPTER SEVEN

"YOU NEVER ANSWERED MY question." William stated once we made it across the bridge and down the other side of the river.

We would be at my aunt's shortly and then we would be halfway through this adventure and I could get away from the ever tempting prince and his tasty dick.

"What question was that?" I stepped over a hard chunk of chocolate along the coast of the river. I didn't know how there was anyone starving in our kingdom with the forest so full of food. Then again, we'd have more obese citizens if they all braved the forest and I would be out of the candy business.

His hand clamped down on my shoulder, jerking me to a stop. "Why do you need me to come with you if you can protect yourself?" His eyes narrowed, suspicion creeping into his expression.

I shrugged, flipping my hair over my shoulder. "Maybe I wanted the company?" My lips curled up into a smirk. "Or maybe I wanted to make sure that you didn't go off and make your condition worse."

"Do you think I'm such a horndog that I cannot control myself?" he stepped closer to me, his gaze boring into me. "I do not need a keeper."

Shifting until my toes bumped against his shoes, I ignored his erection poking me in the stomach. I knew by now that it wasn't because of me. I swiped some lingering chocolate on the side of his lips, bringing it to my mouth and slowly licking it off with a long, drawn-out moan. The prince's tongue shot out and licked the spot I had touched, his eyes darkening with each swipe of my tongue.

With one last satisfying moan of delight, I stepped back from him. "Right. You have all kinds of self-control."

I spun on my heel to walk away, hoping he would watch my ass as I left. A hand clamped on the back of my neck and jerked me back around to him until our noses bumped against one another.

"You are playing a dangerous game, witch." His breath was hot on my lips and it took everything in me not to lean forward and close that distance between us. His next words reminded me why that was a terrible idea. "I wouldn't fuck your filthy cunt if it was the only way to undo my curse."

My hand swung out without thinking. Stinging pain seared through my palm as it connected with the side of his face. William's head flung to the side. His eyes burned into me with more hate than I'd ever seen on another person's face, directed at me.

It was heavy, and I almost regretted hitting him. Was this what my grandmother felt when the village came calling for her head?

I didn't like it.

Not one to go back once having started something, I finished with, "Be careful what you wish for."

Then I spun on my heel and stalked away. Not caring if he followed me or not.

Why did what he said bother me so much? It wasn't like I wanted to have sex with him. He didn't have to be such a dick about it, though.

People not liking me wasn't exactly something new. My grandmother had made sure of that. Not that mom helped things. She should have taught me how to blend in better. How to not be so...me.

I stopped and placed my hands on my hips and scowled. What was I thinking? Me? Change? Why would I change who I am for any of those selfish, ignorant, idiot villagers? I was a bad ass witch and I didn't change for anyone.

"Are we going or what?" Prince William, the fucking tool, shoved by me.

I ignored the tingling where his arm had bumped mine, glaring daggers into his broad back.

No. I didn't need to change. Least of all for him.

We walked in silence for a while.

Thank the gods we didn't encounter any more creatures or you know...him. That was the last thing I needed right now. I had one overbearing asshole male to deal with already. Quota for the day filled.

The prince broke the silence by asking, "What are we getting from this relative of yours again?"

"Well, Willie," I almost smiled at the way his jaw tightened at the nickname. "I need an old-fashioned cauldron and a curse breaking book that my aunt happens to have."

"You don't have a cauldron?" His brows furrowed. "But I thought all witches had cauldrons?"

I snorted, crossing my arms and scuffing my boot against the dirt. "That shows what you know about witches."

William gave me a sideways look. "Then enlighten me."

I stepped up to him and flicked his nose. "No. You don't get to ask me questions after being such a massive dick to me and I don't mean the one in your pants." I forced my eyes to stay on his face and not to stray to that impressive length tenting his pants. "No. If you want to know something, ask nicely and say please."

William gritted his teeth. The effort not to attack me was clear in the straining of his muscles. "Please," he bit out. "Teach me more about witches."

"There we go. Was that so hard?" I patted his cheek with a smirk before starting our journey once again.

William stalked after me a few moments later, the rage in his presence thick enough to make me shudder.

Thinking I probably shouldn't push my luck much more, I explained, "Witches, just like normal humans, come in many varieties. There are so many layers to witches. You can't just judge us all by one person." I continued with a shake of my head, "Some like to ingrain themselves into everyday society, pretending to be healers or apothecaries. Others, like my aunt and myself, prefer to stay separate, preferring not to mingle with normal humans."

"I wonder why," the prince muttered.

I ignored him and continued, "Just like we come in different types, we all need different tools for our craft. Since I tend to focus on the more edible variety."

"Except when you're cursing princes."

I shot him a warning look this time. "I don't need a cauldron. My aunt focuses more on the alternative arts."

"Alternative?"

I smiled. "You'll see."

We walked around the bend, my aunt's house coming into view.

It was strange to step onto the soft dark brown sand of Chocolate Bay. Whenever I thought of my aunt's house, I always thought of the crunch of the vanilla snow beneath my feet. The cool air nipped at my cheeks and nose. Not the warm balm of the forest and trickle of the Milky Way River.

At least her house was the same.

Unlike my grandmother, who made her house out of every delicious pastry and candy imaginable, my aunt was more of a traditionalist. A rickety shack with a crooked chimney puffed black smoke into the air. Her garden sprawled wildly around her home, vines crawling up the sides of the gray piling paint on the sides of the house. I had always wondered if she chose her home for the aesthetics or because she was too lazy to deal with it.

"Well..." the prince trailed off, his eyes taking in everything before him. "This is certainly different."

"See," I skipped forward with a smug grin. "Layers."

The prince sniffed, "Yeah. Like an onion."

I didn't have a chance to get out a clever retort. The door to my aunt's house flew open and she came zipping out on her broomstick, her hand glowing with malicious intent.

"Watch out, Tara. There's a hateful aura coming from that one." Step aside and I will zap him for you."

I had to admit. I was tempted. Tempted to let my aunt transform the prince into something nasty and slimy. It would certainly bring him down a few pegs. At the last moment, I stepped between them and held my hands up before me.

"Hold up there, auntie."

Aunt Nutmeg paused mid air and cocked a graying brow at me. "Are you sure, dearie? He might be pretty to look at but mark my words, he wants to stab you with something."

My face heated with the image that came to mind of what exactly the prince would stab me with.

"Yeah. I'm well aware of his feelings toward me," I said dryly, glancing over my shoulder at the prince who seemed equal parts intrigued and worried about our interaction.

My aunt hummed and then jerked her head down once. "Very well." She lowered to the ground, her broom in her hand. "But you let me know if you change your mind."

I smirked at the prince. "Oh, I definitely will."

CHAPTER EIGHT

STEPPING INTO MY AUNT'S house was like stepping into a memory. The stinging smell of bezzlewarts and fragrant mixture of floral fauna boiling in the large black cauldron in the middle of the room filled the air. The wood fire cracked beneath the hanging cauldron, warming the room more than was comfortable.

"So," Aunt Nutmeg began, pushing around us to grab the big spoon on her work table. Several vials and jars were spread out on the wooden table beside her. She mixed the cauldron with one hand and added a few other items with the other. "What brings you to my home? I haven't seen you in months. Did something happen?" Her small brown eyes slid over to the prince and then back to me.

"Why do you think I only want something whenever I come to visit?" I argued, moving over to the table to survey her ingredients. Mortle tail. Pig's feet. Toadstool. I gaped and picked up a sparkling pink and white filled vial. "Is this fairy dust?" I shook it, watching it float around in the glass.

"Be careful with that." She snatched it out of my hands and tucked it into her apron pocket.

"Where did you get it?" I stared at the pocket as if I could burn a hole through it. "Fairy dust is rare. And you do not have the funds to get it."

My aunt sniffed and turned her back on me. "You don't know everything, girl. Where I get my supplies is my business. Why don't you tell me yours so we can both get back to it?"

I jerked my eyes away from the pocket and frowned. "You're certainly in a bad mood."

Before my aunt could answer, the prince walked up beside her. "Now, now, Tara. Don't be so inconsiderate to your dear aunt. She has been through quite an ordeal.

Don't you remember what that shifter said?" He gave a sympathetic look and brushed some invisible lent from my aunt's black frock. "She was just forced to move her home and now here you come barging in wanting something from her. You should be ashamed of yourself." He lifted my aunt's hand and rubbed it with his other one, giving her a charming smile I'd never seen before. "If you were my aunt, I'm not sure I could stay away."

My aunt giggled.

She fucking giggled like a schoolchild.

Her face colored pink and her shoulders bunched up as she smiled prettily back at him. "Oh, you're a slick one aren't you?"

"I do not know what you mean," the prince placed an offended hand on his chest. "I am the utmost sincere in my affections."

I snorted, leaning against the nearby table. "Then why don't you show her your affliction and how exactly you got it?"

William frowned.

My aunt glanced between us, curiosity flickering in her face. "What's this all about, dearie?"

I gestured to the obscene tent in the prince's pants. "If you'd pay attention to more than his pretty face then you would see what the problem is!"

The prince's lips curled up slightly and I realized my mistake. I'd called him pretty. Which was true. He was the prettiest male I'd ever seen with just a hint of danger laced in his eyes.

"Oh by the gods." My aunt gasped and stared blatantly at the evidence of the prince's curse. "Why, I haven't seen something like that since I was... well... younger." As she gazed hungrily down at the prince's package, something tightened in my chest.

I smacked her on the back, jerking her out of her stupor. "He's not the first man to have a huge cock, auntie. Now, can I borrow your cauldron?"

My aunt glanced away from the prince to me, her brows furrowed. "My cauldron? Why do you need my cauldron?"

"Because all of this..." I gestured at his tented pants. "It's a curse."

Frowning, my aunt cocked her head to the side. "Are you sure? Well, that's a shame."

I was half hoping the prince would correct me about his size being part of the curse but he didn't say anything. Instead, he shot me glare. "You would know, you're the one who cursed me."

My aunt gaped. "No wonder he wants to kill you. Tara, what did I tell you about playing with curses? You should stick to your candy making and leave cursing to the professionals."

"I did not curse him," I snapped back. "I sold a variable curse to one of his disgruntled lovers. She made up the curse, not me. I just supplied the ammunition."

"Oh, I've heard of those kinds of curses," My aunt nodded her head solemnly. "They tend to be more harmful than anything we come up with and usually the punishment matches the crime..." Her eyes slid coyly back to the prince's erection. "I'm guessing you charmed your way into one too many ladies' panties, isn't that right lad? Got you with a fidelity curse, she did." My aunt threw her head back and cackled.

"A fidelity curse?" the prince growled. "I wasn't even dating her! Why do you women all think that just because we spend some time together it means that we are committed to you alone?"

My aunt leaned toward me while the prince ranted and whispered, "A playboy that one, huh?"

I bobbed my head. "You have no idea." To the prince, I sighed, "Are you quite finished?

The prince opened his mouth to no doubt give me a snarky remark but my aunt cut in.

"Alright you two, you can harp on each other later. It's late and this old gal wants to go have a nightcap and go to bed. We can handle this tomorrow."

"But your niece assured me this could be taken care of tonight," the prince argued, all attempts at being charming gone.

"You won't be getting nothing from me until I've had my nine hours of sleep. Now, get. There's a spare bed upstairs though there is only one so you'll have to figure out which one of you gets it." The sly look in her eyes told me that she wasn't going to magically make me another bed. Nosy busybody.

The prince looked like he was about to argue again but then clamped his mouth shut. "Very well. I can see I won't be getting what I want tonight. Good night." He stalked up the stairs leaving me alone with my aunt.

Her eyes trailed after the prince until he was gone and the door upstairs snapped shut. Then she turned to me with a grin. "Drink?"

I sank into the nearby chair and sighed, "Yes, please."

She tootled around the room until she brought a glass bottle full of amber liquid and two semi clean glasses to the small table and sat down in the other chair across from me. She poured a generous amount in each glass before pushing one over to me.

"So...this is quite the pickle you've gotten yourself into, dearie," she said over her glass, then sipped from it.

I shrugged, wincing as the liquid burned down my throat. "It's not so bad."

"My wondering is why you're helping him in the first place?" She jerked her head toward the stairs. "He's the prince, if I'm not mistaken, yes?"

I slumped lower in my chair. "Yeah, what about it?"

"Ah," she smiled knowingly, "You always were the romantic type. Had your nose in all those fairy tales growing up."

I narrowed my eyes. "It's not like that. I'm only helping him in exchange for something I want."

"Have you had a chance to, you know...sample the goods?" She wiggled her brows at me.

"No! And I won't be. I am simply helping him fix his problem and then we will go our separate ways."

"Then I don't see what you're getting out of it. If you're not going to bed him then what good is he?" she drained her glass and then leaned forward, her gaze going hard. "He didn't threaten you, did he?"

On multiple occasions, but I didn't tell her that.

"No. And don't worry about it." I wasn't about to tell my aunt I wanted to make candy out of the mold of his dick. She already thought I was weird enough.

She filled her glass back up and leaned back in her chair. "So why don't you tell me about this curse?"

CHAPTER NINE

BY THE TIME I explained what I knew about the curse on William's dick, I was exhausted and a little bit more than tipsy.

I stumbled up the stairs, holding the railing as I went. I wasn't quite to the point where the world was spinning, but I was feeling a lot happier about the prospect of sharing a bed with his majesty and his candy cane dick.

Not bothering to knock, I threw the door open and found the prince sitting on the side of the bed, his cock in his hands. He wasn't stroking himself or doing anything obscene, just staring down at it as if he could change it back to normal.

My mind drifted back to the last time I saw him holding his cock in his hands like that and warmth puddled between my legs. Shoving the desire aside, I approached him, my steps only swaying slightly.

"So... I had a thought..." I flopped down on the bed opposite of him. "You masturbated just fine without the curse spreading."

"Your point?" The prince said from behind me.

I leaned back until I could tip my head back and see him. "So, it should say something about the... the... damn it..." I clicked my tongue and tried to think of the word but my head was too fuzzy.

"The parameters of the curse?" the prince offered, his eyes rolling at my inebriated state.

"Yes," I snapped my fingers. "That."

"Yes, I had considered it. I did a bit of experimenting before it came to this."

I let myself lay back on the bed until my head was next to his hip and his candy cane dick was in view. "So you can get off yourself, but if you have sex with another it causes it to spread?"

"Yes."

"What about oral? Hand stuff? Boob stuff? Kissing?" I started naming off all the other things you could do besides cock to pussy penetration.

"I don't know. I haven't tried it. Any of that stuff leads to fucking for me." His lips curled up on one side.

"So what did you test out?" I stared up at him. "Did you know your lashes are really long?"

Ignoring my observation, the prince put himself back in his pants and shifted to stare down at me. "Exactly what I said. I fucked, and it grew. I masturbated, and it didn't. That makes a difference, but I don't know why."

My lips twitched.

"Say it, just fucking say it. I know you want to."

"For someone who sleeps around as much as you, you don't know anything about women, do you?" I propped myself up on my elbows to look at him closer. "She cursed you because she was upset that you were fucking other women. It's obvious she would only focus on that part of the curse. I doubt she even thought about punishing you for anything else."

He narrowed his eyes. "And how do you know that?"

"Well, there's only one way to find out." I grabbed the back of his neck and jerked his head down to mine, slanting my lips against his plump ones. His facial hair scratched my face deliciously, and I leaned into the kiss.

William took longer to respond.

I expected him to shove me away with another bout of the whole filthy cunt bit but he surprised me by curling his fingers around the back of my neck and pressing his lips harder against mine.

A low groan released from me.

The prince jerked back. The confusion and regret on his face may have made me feel bad about kissing him, but the desire heating his eyes held it back.

"Well?" I licked my lips and eyed down at his pants. "Did it change any?"

He blinked as if forgetting the reason we had kissed in the first place. No pulling his dick back out, he glanced down into his pants where the candy cane coating stopped at the top of his pubic hair. "No. It didn't move at all."

"I rest my case." Pushing up off the bed, I bent over to take my shoes off. The world spun, and I groaned for another reason. "I think I'm going to puke."

William sighed and the bed shifted. The prince knelt before me and threw my hands away from my shoes. "Sit up. I don't want to smell puke all night long." Without asking, he untied my boots and pulled them off my feet.

I stared at him kneeling before me, and my body flushed with the need to kiss him again.

Why was I getting all worked up? It was just a kiss. Not even that good of one. There wasn't even any tongue.

I cleared my throat. "Thank you." Then I lifted my fingers to the buttons of my dress and popped each one out of their confines, my eyes still on the prince.

"What are you doing?" his eyes followed my fingers.

I shrugged. "I'm hot and I'm not sleeping in this dress. If you don't like it you can sleep outside for all I care."

William's eyes shot up and he stood to his feet, that bite in his voice coming back. "I'm the crown prince. I do not sleep outside like some commoner. You go sleep outside."

"Nope," I popped, pushing the last button out of its hole before shifting to lower the top of my dress. "This is my aunt's house. I'm sleeping in here."

The prince's eyes dipped to where my chemise covered my chest, my moderately sized boobs probably in need of a corset, but I'd always refused to tie my puppies down. The ladies needed to breathe, and no one cared what a witch wore, anyway. However, my decision not to wear one had my nipples straining against the cotton fabric and the prince's gaze locked onto them.

I stood, putting myself chest to chest with the prince. I shimmied out of the dress until it dropped to the floor. The chemise landed just below my butt, leaving my legs bare. "There's plenty of room in the bed. We could share."

The prince's eyes dipped to take them in before they shot back up to my face. Something tightened in his expression and he snapped, "Fine." He stalked over to his side of the bed and pulled his shirt over his head. "Just keep your hands to yourself, witch."

I made myself not drool over his muscled chest and dryly stated, "I'll try to restrain myself."

Slipping into the bed, I forced my eyes onto the ceiling and not the prince untying his boots, letting each one thud to the ground. For a moment, I held my breath half hoping and half worried he was going to take his pants off and get in the bed naked. When he slid into the bed next to me still wearing his pants, I blew out the breath I held.

Immediately, he turned his back to me, unable or not wanting to look at me while he slept. I listened to his breathing, waiting for him to fall asleep. Why had I suggested this? His body heat came off of him in waves and I was very much aware of every movement on his side of the bed. I was almost afraid to move in case I accidentally brushed against him.

I let my eyes wander over to the prince's back, tracing over the curves of his muscles. A tattoo decorated the top left side of his shoulder. A bird with spread wings, broken chains wrapped around them. In its claws was a snake. I wanted to reach out and touch it. My fingers were halfway there when his voice rang out.

"Stop staring at me."

My eyes jerked back to the ceiling. "What's your tattoo mean?"

William was quiet for a long moment before he answered. "That even in the binds of my position, I am still free and I will rip into those who tried to chain me down."

I arched my brow. "And I thought it was just me you were so violent with."

"There are more than a few who would see me harmed or seek to manipulate me for their own gains. The tattoo is a reminder that I am my own person or something like that. I was barely sixteen when I received it and arrogant as all hell."

I snorted a laugh. "More so than now?"

He chuckled darkly. "Perpetually more so."

"I feel sorry for your teachers."

"Don't be. We paid them more than handsomely for putting up with me, and without several of them, I would have been considerably worse than I am now."

I shook my head and turned on my side, giving up the pretense that I wasn't looking at him. "I can't imagine you worse than now."

William shifted until he turned on his other side and we were face to face. "If not for my tutors, I would not have come to you to undo the curse, I would have called in all the witches and magical beings in the area. Killing anyone that failed to fix me."

I balked. "That's a bit extreme. Don't you think so?"

He shrugged. "Not much more extreme than cursing your onetime lover's dick for not being committed to you alone."

I snorted. "That's debatable."

CHAPTER TEN

I'D NEVER HAD SUCH a good night's sleep. My bed wasn't uncomfortable per se. There was just something about my aunt's bed. It's so warm and cozy and...poking me in the butt.

My entire body stiffened. I didn't even breathe. I opened my eyes, praying to whatever deity was listening that the heavy warm object wrapped around my waist was not an arm and the thing cupping my breast was not a hand.

I'd never been a very religious person and this was them punishing me, wasn't it?

Slowly, I twisted my head to peek over my shoulder. Prince William's face sat two inches from mine, his breath warm against my face. I took a moment to notice the way his long eyelashes lay on cheek. The line of his nose, my eyes dipping down until you get to his lips. Those full bitable lips.

Why was he so fucking delicious?

It's no wonder someone cursed him. If I was in their position I would want to keep him too and I haven't even slept with him yet!

Wait. Yet? There will be no yet. He's an incorrigible pain in the ass. I had my dignity and pride. Or well sort of. Besides, he didn't want anything to do with me.

As if sensing my thoughts, the hand cupping my breast squeezed slightly, his thumb circling over my nipple until it pebbled. He pulled it tight between his fingers and I almost bit through my lip to keep my moan at bay.

This had to stop. He was going to wake up and see that it's me he was groping and then he'd do the whole threatening thing again.

But then he let out a low growly moan and his hips thrust against me. When he couldn't find an opening, he shifted his hips and his enormous cock pressed its way between my thighs, rubbing against me until my panties were soaked through.

Oh fuck. This was wrong. This was oh so wrong. I had to stop it. I had to stop it now.

I opened my mouth to do just that when the hand groping my breast dragged down between my legs and deviled beneath the fabric covering me. Two fingers expertly circled and teased my clit until my eyes rolled into the back of my head. It was coming. I was going to…and he wasn't even awake to know he had done it.

That was a bucket of cold water on me.

"Geez, Willie, if you wanted to fuck me all you had to do was ask." I retorted haughtily and hoped he didn't hear the husky way my voice had changed.

The man behind me completely froze. I wasn't even sure he was breathing anymore by how stiff he had become.

A deep throaty voice asked, "Witch?" His hand and cock still sat between my legs, not moving, and that was a special kind of torture I would think about later.

I let the smile on my face grow so he could hear it in my voice. "Yep."

"Fuck," he cursed and jerked his hand and cock away so fast I wondered if they ripped some flesh off in the process. The bed shifted and I rolled on my other side, leaning up on my hand to smirk at him.

"Why didn't you stop me?" he snarled, pulling shirt on and fastening the buttons.

I shrugged. "Call it morbid curiosity." I let my gaze linger over him. "You know, I can sort of see the appeal now. That was quite a show you put on there. I almost forgot you're an arrogant man whore."

The prince stalked back to the bed and I readied myself for what was likely another threat on my life. He grabbed the back of my neck and jerked me toward him until I could feel his cock digging into my thigh.

"I don't think it was curiosity at all. I think you liked it." His voice was low and threatening, his mouth so close to mine I could kiss him if I just leaned slightly forward.

"Don't kid yourself," I bit back. "I wouldn't want to catch what you have. I hear candy cane dick is spreading."

Without warning, his other hand went between my thighs and cupped me through my panties. "You're such a nasty little liar. You're completely soaked. I bet you were just seconds away from coming on my hand and candy cane dick, weren't you, witch?"

I didn't answer him.

If he touched my clit now, I would explode. I just knew it.

"Weren't you, Tara?" His hand pressed against the aching part of me and I let out a breathy moan.

Fuck. The combination of his hand and my name on his lips was too much for me. A small quake went through my body, not enough to satisfy my body but enough that my eyes flicked open and I saw the same expression I'd given him just moments ago.

I ground my pussy against his hand and murmured, "It's just a physical reaction, Willie. Don't think you're so special."

His jaw clenched and for a moment I thought he was going to kiss me before he ripped himself away and stalked out of the room, the door slamming behind him.

I sank back against the headboard with a long, shuddering breath.

I was in so much trouble. We almost. I almost.

Dragging a hand down my face, I let it rest on my neck for a moment, remembering the feel of his hand on me. That, of course, made the rest of me remember his hands in other places and my body was raring to go once more.

If I didn't get rid of some of this tension, I wasn't going to last the whole trip to Bianca's and back. I'd jump on the prince, candy cane dick or not, and ride it until we both hated ourselves afterward.

My eyes flicked to the door, and I cocked my head to the side, listening for anyone coming. My aunt's and the prince's muffled voices came from downstairs. I had time.

Dropping my hand to my still soaked panties, I made quick work of circling my clit as I cupped and pinched my nipple just the way the prince had a few moments ago. I closed my eyes, my breathing coming in short pants now as I came closer to that edge.

It wasn't enough.

Something was missing.

His enormous cock, of course.

I plunged three fingers into my core, not bothering to prep myself for it. The stinging pressure was just what I imagined it would feel like to have him inside of me. Soon the pressure changed into another kind and my inner muscles were clenching around my fingers, my toes curling and my spine lifting up off the bed as I orgasmed.

Clamping a hand over my mouth, I let myself ride it until I came shakily back down to the bed.

My gaze shifted to the door once more before I quickly cleansed and dressed myself. My legs felt wobbly, and I wasn't at all satiated. Nope. My body wanted one thing and one thing only and it was standing on the other side of the door with his arms and legs crossed and a shit-eating grin on his face.

Fuck me.

"Are you ready to go?" I brushed past him, ignoring the fact that he most likely knew exactly what I had been doing just a few moments ago.

"Well, we know you are." Prince William grabbed my wrist and crowded around me until he had me back up against the wall, his mouth close to my ear. "And for future reference. You're going to need four fingers, not three, to get close to ready for my size."

I gaped at his back as he walked away.

Everything I had just done a few minutes ago went straight out the window. My body was hot and ready to go once more and that fucking bastard knew it.

This wouldn't do.

He was the one who came begging me for help. Okay, more like threatening me for help, but still. I could very well leave him the way he was, not getting off by anyone other than his hand for the rest of his life or turning into a full fledged candy cane man when he couldn't take it anymore.

I was going to show Prince William. He didn't know who he was messing with. He was about to find out, though.

CHAPTER ELEVEN

MY AUNT USED HER magic to float her back up cauldron into the room. When she sat it down, it dropped like a stone, cracking the wooden board beneath it. She chuckled faintly. "Oops, I slipped."

The prince eyeballed the cauldron. "How are you going to carry this to your friend's house and back?"

Still mad at him, I waved a hand, and the cauldron began to shrink in size until it was big enough to tuck into my pocket.

"Oh."

I cocked a brow. "Any other stupid questions?"

A dark expression flashed across William's face for a moment, and then seemed to remember my aunt in the room. Instead, he turned to her with a charming grin. "Thank you so much for your hospitality. It will not be forgotten."

"Now you take care now, your highness and don't be a stranger." Aunt Nutmeg smacked the prince on the chest with a dish towel, blushing like a schoolchild.

"Please," William lifted her hand and kissed it, "William. Only those idiots at court call me your highness."

"Oh, you." She swatted at him again and then eyed me over her shoulder. "You be careful with this one, you hear me, dearie? He'll have your drawers off you before you even know what's happening."

The prince smirked at me behind my aunt's back.

I clenched my jaw. "I know."

The prince gave my aunt one more charming smile before walking out of the house. I paused there, staring at him, wondering how he would look with a licorice rope twisted around his neck.

"You like him."

My head jerked around. "What? No, I don't."

Aunt Nutmeg wiped her hands on the towel and sat down at the table, picking up her teacup. "You're glaring at him so hard your eyes are popping out of your head."

I snorted. "See? I clearly hate the man. Besides, his dick got cursed because he's such a man whore. Why would I even want to be in the same room as him? There's a reason I avoid the village and especially the castle. Those people hate us. They don't understand us. Look what they did to grandma!"

Aunt Nutmeg opened her mouth, but I cut her off.

"Yeah, yeah, I know she tried to eat those kids, but still. You have to admit, his kind has not been kind to ours. No." I shook my head, more to convince myself than her. "I couldn't possibly like that overbearing, self-centered asshole."

"If you say so, dearie." Aunt Nutmeg sipped from her cup so calmly it was maddening.

"I do say so." I grabbed the front door handle and paused. "We're going to fix his dick and then I'm going to go back to my life. Away from humans and exactly how I like it."

I slammed the door behind me for good measure.

"Is everything alright?" the prince asked once I was outside.

"Let's go," I snapped, stalking away from my aunt's house.

For a while, I thought I was out of the woods. Physically and metaphorically. William didn't say another word about what had happened at my aunt's as we headed into the licorice swamp and the idea of wrapping one of those vines around the prince's neck stayed in the forefront of my mind.

I almost relaxed.

Then he opened his big mouth.

"So... tell me." William strolled alongside me. "Was I as good as you thought?'

My fingers tightened into fists. Then I relaxed and smiled. "No. It left me woefully unsatisfied."

"Oh, really now," he continued with a thoughtful pinch of his lips. "It looked to me like you reached completion easily enough."

"That's only because I was thinking of Percy at the end. Now he knows how to satisfy a woman." I chuckled to myself, having no idea, in fact, what Percy was like in bed. Apparently, it riled the prince up enough that he grabbed my arm, jerking us to a stop.

"Do not lie to me. You were not thinking about that dog while you were finger fucking yourself." Gripping my other arm so that I couldn't pull away from him. He leaned closer and growled, "You were thinking about me."

I pressed up on my toes and lifted my lips to ghost across his, the urge to lick those bitable lips almost too much to hold back. I did though and whispered, "Nope."

He released me with a snarl and stalked forward.

"You know if you hadn't been peeking, then you wouldn't even be bothered by this. Besides," I trailed after him happily, watching his butt cheeks clench and unclench, "weren't you the one who said you wouldn't touch me if it were the only way to break your curse?"

"That's not what I said and you know it." William quipped, spinning around to walk backward. "I said I wouldn't fuck —" his words cut off as he fell, his scream following in his wake.

My heart jumped into my throat and I hurried over to the side of the pit, peering over the edge. "William!"

"I'm fine," he grunted from six feet down. "I think I just broke my..." he adjusted himself in his pants and winced. "Candy cane."

I covered my mouth with a laugh.

"Yes, it's very funny." He crawled to his feet and stared up at the slippery brown sides of the pit. "Now, can you find something to get me out of here, or can you do that magic thing your aunt did and lift me out?"

"Sorry, can't. That only works on inanimate objects." I moved back from the edge, not wanting to fall in with him, and searched for a long enough licorice vine to throw down to him.

"You know your magic isn't very consistent," he called up from the pit. "It can do some things but not other things. I thought you were all powerful. At least, that's how you seemed when you were wrangling that shifter."

I grabbed a long black rope of licorice, tugging it to make sure it wouldn't break, and then shrugged. Then remembered he couldn't see me. "Different witches can do different things. And I am not even close to all powerful. I knew Percy wouldn't hurt me. He likes it when I hurt him too much."

"I'm not sure if that's comforting or not."

I tied one end of the licorice around a nearby tree and then looped the other side around my arm. "Either way, you don't have anything to worry about. We'll get you home and candy cane free in no time. Then you can go back to fucking all the ladies in the kingdom. Here, catch." I tossed the loose end over the edge.

"Uh... yes, right. I have lots of time to make up for." William wrapped one end around his hand and propped his feet up on the wall. "Are you sure this is sturdy? It's not going to snap, is it?"

I grinned down at him. "Not unless you take a big bite out of it."

"That sounds like an excellent idea."

I jerked away from the pit. My foot slipped, and I was careening over the side. William's voice shouted, "Tara!"

A pale red, almost pink hand shot out and grabbed my arm. Nails bit into my flesh and I was pressed up against a hard concave chest. My nose filled with the smell of tobacco and a faint coppery scent.

I recognized that smell.

My eyes trailed over the form fitting jacket and gold cufflinks. His thick neck, so pale his veins could be seen beneath the surface, flexed as he swallowed.

I swallowed thickly, lifting my head to meet the dark red gaze of my savior and future demise. "Hello, Blackthorn."

His thin wine colored lips, curled into a feral fanged smile. "Hello, my precious."

CHAPTER TWELVE

IF THE VILLAGERS REALLY knew what roamed their woods at night they wouldn't be so quick to judge me and my kind. There were fates far worse than being cooked and eaten.

Like being the immortal bride of the creature holding me.

My heart sputtered in my chest for a whole different reason now. One that had nothing to do with the prince and everything to do with the vampire before me.

"What are you doing here, my precious?" Blackthorn murmured, his bright red hair falling over his forehead as he stroked the side of my face with one long black fingernail.

I held back a wince. They were sharp but he didn't press hard enough to pierce the skin.

I forced my breathing to slow. To not give him any indication that I feared him as much as I did.

Right now, Blackthorn still wanted to fuck me, to make me one of his little brides. Which was never going to happen, but I did not want to be on Blackthorn's list of food prospects either.

"I'm helping out a disgruntled customer," I stated, relieved my voice didn't come out as shaky as I felt.

The prince still worked on getting out of the pit and part of me wished he would take his time. I did not want Blackthorn to meet William.

Blackthorn cocked his head, his pointed ears twitching while he listened. "Why don't you let me take care of that for you?" His cold lips brushed against my cheek. "Consider it a wedding gift."

My eyes widened and I disentangled myself from him. "No. No. Thank you, but no. I don't want to get the reputation of killing my customers or I won't have any left." I gave a nervous chuckle.

Blackthorn's lips twitched on one side, not quite a smile but enough to show his amusement.

He circled me with watchful eyes. "When are you going to stop this whole game of shopkeeper and come be my bride?" Lifting my thick curly hair away from my neck, he trailed his nose along my throat, inhaling deeply. "You would want for nothing and live forever. It would be a pity to lose such a beautiful woman to the ravages of time."

My breath came out in a shudder. "Oh, you know me. Work, work, work. And besides, I'm not that old. I have plenty of time left before I get old and wrinkly. Some even say we get more beautiful with age."

"I prefer mine young and supple," Blackthorn practically groaned in my ear. A whimper escaped me and I clamped my lips shut.

"I will ask you politely to unhand my witch."

When I hear the prince's voice, I nearly yell at him to run.

It was too late for running.

Too late for a lot of things.

"Ah, this must be the disgruntled customer," Blackthorn mused. "I can see why you don't want me to take care of him for you." He released me and gave me a look of disapproval before slithering toward William. "And who might you be?"

I rushed to jump between them. "He's nobody and no one. One of his many lovers cursed him for being unfaithful and I'm simply trying to fix it. Nothing else to it."

"Cursed is it?" Blackthorn pushed me aside, more gently than expected from him. I watched with bated breath as the vampire surveyed the prince from his roguish good looks to the expensive clothing and lastly settling in the ever prominent evidence of his curse. "I would not find such a state to be a curse if I were in your position."

"You would if you were going to end up a living candy cane by the end," William sneered. "And you are not me."

Blackthorn flashed his fangs. "That we can agree on."

I moved once more to get between the two of them. Blackthorn flicked his wrist and several licorice vines wrapped around me. Tight enough to restrict my movements but not enough to suffocate me.

"Now, now, my precious. We are just getting to know one another." He smacked his lips as he said each word. "How rude of me not to introduce myself. I am Blackthorn, ruler of the Licorice Swamp and Tara's betrothed. Who may you be?"

William arched a brow at Blackthorn before saying to me. "Just how many beaus do you have? First Percy and now this one? Do they know something about you I don't?"

I glared at him. "I will have you know others find me utterly irresistible."

"Enough." Blackthorn interrupted us. "I am the only beau my precious has. That mutt is a delusional nuisance." He poked William in the chest with a sharp black fingernail. "Now. Who are you?"

I squinted my eyes and tried to push my thoughts at the prince. Hoping he would be smart enough not to tell Blackthorn who he really was. Unfortunately, I was not gifted with the ability of telepathy.

"You stand before your prince. William of Candiopolis." He stated with as much arrogance as was befitting a royal.

If Blackthorn was surprised he didn't show it. His bright red brows lifted as if coming to some conclusion. "Ah, I see it now. I knew your father." Blackthorn smirked and trailed a nail across the left side of his cheek. "Does he still carry my scar?"

William's face colored with rage. "You are the one who did that to him? He said he received it fighting for his life on the battlefield."

Blackthorn smiled delightfully. "What is not love if not a battlefield?"

I frowned.

I'd never heard of this.

"Oh, do not be cross with me, my precious. I have lived a long time and there have been many brides before you. Forever does get lonely." To the prince, Blackthorn said, "Your father was in the same position as you are right now. Though, it was for his sister rather than his lover."

"You're what happened to Aunt Sylvia?" William gaped at him with horror.

"She is one of many. But sadly passed on. Immortality did not suit her."

"I am not his lover," I refuted, dragging his attention back to me. I twisted against the vines. They were so damn tight! "So you have no quarrel with him."

Blackthorn pursed his lips. "You say so but your scent does not lie." He inhaled deeply, a sort of sigh leaving his lips as he breathed out. "The scent of your arousal is prominent and all over him." He gestured to the prince.

"That was..." I swallowed and looked off to the side, "...a misunderstanding."

Blackthorn snarled. "Did this piece of filth touch you against your will? I will cut off his cock and then the curse will not matter."

"No. No." I quickly denied. "It wasn't like that."

Blackthorn's face turned solemn. "So it was consensual."

My gaze shot from Blackthorn to William and back. "It was not not nonconsensual."

"You are trying to confuse me and I am not amused." Blackthorn sighed and shook his head. "It is my fault. I have let you go on with your life without daily reminders of who you belong to." He shrugged his shoulders and straightened. "Nevertheless. That is something I will be sure to remedy after I have dealt with his highness."

"You will not handle me," William snapped, not knowing when to keep his mouth shut. "You will release the witch and let us be on our way or I will have your head."

I froze.

Blackthorn was not one for idle threats. He was sure to counter the prince with a threat of his own and I couldn't have that.

I didn't know why but the idea of the prince dying at the hands of Blackthorn made my eyes burn. I struggled stronger against the vine. If I could only get my mouth close to them then I could chew through them.

Blackthorn had done his tying well. None of the vines were even close to where I could get to them without contorting myself in ways that I might not live from. It only proves further than he had done this many times before.

Unfortunately, I didn't have time to ponder how I was going to get out of this one and save the prince without him knowing I gave two gummy bear asses about him. Blackthorn had made his decision.

"To prove I am a malevolent creature, I will make you a deal." Blackthorn's eyes flicked over to me before going back to the prince. "Give up your claim on my precious heart and I won't rip yours from your chest. You can even go home with a matching scar to show your father."

CHAPTER THIRTEEN

TO WILLIAM'S CREDIT, HE didn't flinch back or cower before Blackthorn's threat. He stood his ground and stared Blackthorn's evil eyes down.

"Well, now, your highness, do we have a deal?" Blackthorn flashed a fang toothed smile.

William opened his mouth to respond but I beat him to it.

"There is... nothing... to make a deal... about," I grunted, pushing and pulling against the vines. I could not let my prince... I mean my customer... get killed on my watch. It was bad enough that I had to deal with the outcome of the curse I sold, if he died on my watch...

I couldn't stomach the thought.

"Now, my precious." Blackthorn hissed, stepping away from the prince to face me. He put his back to the prince which was either a trick or he really wasn't worried about William coming at him. "I will not have anyone standing between you and our love. It will last an... eternity." I flinched away from the clawed finger stroking the side of my face.

"I don't know where you ever got it into your head that I would ever want to be with you," I grit out, shoving him back with my bound body. "You can't start a fight with him over something that doesn't exist!"

"Oh, precious." Blackthorn clasped his hand over his chest. "You only need time to see that there is no one else in this world more perfect for you than me. And to make sure that you see..." he spun around and William's fist smashed into his face.

"Never touch her again," William growled, slamming his fist into Blackthorn's face again.

My panties exploded.

Never had a man come to my defense like the prince was right then.

Sure I could take care of myself.

I had all my life.

The fact that William had stood up for me and not taken the easy way out when he clearly despised me, made me want to jump on his candy cane cock and ride it until we ended up in a sticky mess.

Blackthorn swiped his hand under his nose, licking the blood off his hand. "Very well, your highness. You have drawn first blood. Let the best man win. But I warn you, it will be me."

If William was worried he didn't show it. He lifted his fists once more, watching the vampire as he stalked toward him.

Fortunately, Blackthorn was too preoccupied by William and had completely forgotten about me for the moment, giving me the chance to figure out a way out of my tight bonds.

Reluctantly, I tore my eyes away from the fight, searching the ground and air for something that might cut the candy ropes around me.

Fuck what I wouldn't give for a knife right about now.

My eyes lit up.

Or a sharp rock. That would do.

Awkwardly, I bent at the knees, trying to angle my body so that I could grab the rock. My eyes kept moving back to Blackthorn and William. I winced at each blow William took to the face, each scrape of the vampire's claws against him.

Blackthorn might have the advantage with his claws and fangs but William was holding his own... for now.

My fingers curled around the cool surface of the stone, the edges of it biting in my palm. I twisted the rock until I could press it against the licorice ropes. Sawing at the candy, I glanced up just in time to see Blackthorn slash William across the upper thigh.

I cried out and sawed harder at the ropes. They barely budged. Groaning with frustration, I tightened my hand around the rock until I knew it would leave indents in my palm.

"Need a bit of help?"

My head jerked up. "Percy?"

I had never been happier to see the shifter than right that second.

Still shirtless but wearing pants now, Percy popped out from behind a tree. His dark red eyes flicked over to where the others were fighting and then back to me. "So, I see your new boyfriend met your old one."

"He is not my boyfriend," I snarled, twisting around to face him. "None of you are or ever have been. Now, are you going to help me or not?"

Percy smirked and licked his lips. "Maybe...for a price."

I gaped at the shifter. "Serious-fucking-ly? You're going to try to extort me right now?"

Shrugging, Percy fingered the ropes wrapped around me. "Well, you're tied up at the moment, when am I ever going to get this chance again?" He leaned into me, his fangs pulling on his lower lip.

When I opened my mouth to tell him to go fuck himself, William shouted in pain. The chokehold the prince had the vampire in didn't work well for someone who didn't need to breathe. Now, William fought against Blackthorn's head where the vampire had his fangs plunged into the prince's arm. The more blood that poured out of William's wounds the more my heart thudded in my chest.

I turned back to Percy and croaked out, "Yes. Okay. Whatever you want. Just get me out of here so I can help him."

Percy pursed his lips and frowned, his eyes darting to the prince and then back to me as if he were contemplating helping him... or Blackthorn, I couldn't tell which.

Finally, Percy turned back to me, his lips pinched tight as he pointed a finger at me. "You owe me one after this."

Not waiting for my reply, he sliced through the ropes with his claws.

I shoved the ropes off of me, not pausing to thank Percy before darting to William's aid.

With the rock still clenched in my fist, I swung my hand down and smashed it into Blackthorn's face again and again until he finally let go of William's arm and turned on me with a snarl, blood dripping from his open mouth.

"Precious, you go too far." His words came out a gurgling hiss.

"Not yet, I haven't..." I lifted my arm above my head and let it fly. This time when rock hit Blackthorn's face something cracked and he went down hard. I dropped the rock and grabbed onto William's good arm, slinging it over my shoulder.

"Come on, your highness. You can't die here." I grunted and hauled the heavier-than-he-looked prince up to his feet. "I do not want to know what kind of reputation that would get me."

"Heh," William grunted and laughed. "It couldn't get worse than what it is now."

"You two can contemplate your latest review after we get away from the vengeful vampire," Percy snapped, grabbing William's other arm and taking the brunt of the weight.

"Where should we go?" I glanced around us. There wasn't exactly a physician in the middle of the forest who could take care of the prince. "He's going to need to be bandaged up."

William scoffed, rolling his head toward me. "Nah, it's not that bad. See..." he tried to lift himself on his own but the blood loss was too much for him and he fell face first into the ground.

I sighed, my hands on my hips and then gestured at the prone prince. "Well, this is just great."

Percy frowned down at the prince and then scratched the side of his head. "Yes, this does put us in quite the predicament." He crossed his arms over his chest and twisted his lips to the side in thought. "There is a place you could take him. It's not much. More of a hole than a dwelling. But it will get him out of harm's way for the moment until you can get him patched up."

"I don't really have much of a choice in the matter," I glared back at Blackthorn's form. "And we can't stay here. Blackthorn is a pain in the ass when he likes me, I can only imagine how he will feel about me now that I knocked him the fuck out."

Chuckling, Percy knelt down and lifted William into his arms. He made that look so easy. "If the vampire is anything like me, it will make him want you even more." He winked at me and strode forward, leaving me lagging behind and wondering what the hell I did to deserve this.

CHAPTER FOURTEEN

WHEN PERCY SAID THE place was more of a hole, he hadn't been understating it. The place was a literal hole in the wall barely big enough for us to crawl into one at a time and with no light at the end.

I conjured a ball of light and squinted into the abyss.

"How far down does it go?" I asked, tempted to run back out the other way. I didn't want something creepy and crawly to sneak up on us. More specifically something with teeth.

Percy shrugged, handing me the prince through the hole. "Don't know."

My eyes widened. "You don't know? What if something lives here? It could be a snake's nest or worse!"

Crawling in after the prince, Percy shook his head. "Nah, I've stayed here a lot of times to get out of the storms. Nothing has ever come out of the dark."

"That's not at all comforting," I muttered to myself as I propped the prince up a bit harder on the wall than I meant to.

William groaned.

"Sorry," I winced, my hands up to catch him if he slipped. I moved closer to the prince and inspected his wounds. The one on his thigh wasn't too concerning. It was barely more than a scratch, though it would probably leave a scar.

It was the one on his arm that was worrying. Blackthorn hadn't just bit into the prince, he had gnawed at him like a wild animal, his skin torn until muscle and bone showed through.

My face feeling flushed, I turned to Percy. "I don't think I can do much for him. He needs more help than I can provide."

"It's that bad?"

I nodded.

"Well... I guess you don't have to worry about fixing his curse now," Percy chuckled halfheartedly, earning a glare from me. "Alright, I get it. You like the prince. I won't let him die." He muttered something else under his breath but I didn't catch it.

"What was that?" I asked, my tone filled with warning. I wouldn't let Percy's jealousy be the death of William. I was better than that.

"Nothing," Percy stayed crouched near the doorway, if you could call it that. "I said, I'll go for help if you can keep him alive until I get back."

I licked my lips and shook my head, my stomach twisting into knots. "I can staunch the bleeding... keep it clean but I don't have any tools to sew him up."

"Then do what you can," Percy propped one foot up on the hole's opening. "I'll be back with help as soon as I can."

Then he was gone before I could ask who exactly Percy was getting help from.

Left alone with the prince, I chewed on my lower lip. Patching up people was not in my bag of skills. I barely had a bag of skills, but sewing people up was definitely not one of them.

Swallowing down the nervousness in my stomach, I crawled across the ground toward William. His eyes were partly slit open, following my every movement.

"You know, I imagined you just like this..." William grunted and winced. "But I was in a lot less pain and of course not bleeding out."

My face heated and I nudged him in the chest. "That's not funny. You could have died...you still could." I leaned over his wound, poking at the edges where blood leaked out. Thankfully it wasn't coming out too fast, the saliva in a vampire's bite made the blood slow to give them time to feed properly.

"That hurts, you know." William flinched away from my touch.

"Sorry." My face pinched together as I went about ripping the lace off the bottom of my skirt. "You shouldn't have done that."

"Done what?" William arched his brow. "Defend your honor?"

"What honor would that be?" I snorted, pulling the trimming out and looping it around William's arm. "Besides, what's it to you? You hate me."

"I wouldn't say that."

I could feel his eyes on me while I wrapped the lace around his arm until it was short enough to tie. "Then what would you say? That I'm a filthy witch who irresponsibly gives out curses to anyone who gives her money." I tightened the knot with each word, gritting my teeth until my jaw hurt.

"You know, I think my arm is all better now." William shifted a bit too quickly out of my reach, his hands stopping mine from tightening the lace even more.

"Shit. I didn't mean..." I rubbed my forehead and slumped down on the ground next to him. "I'm just making everything worse, aren't I?" Placing my head in my lap, I pushed back the angry tears that threatened to fall.

I would not cry in front of him. I would not cry. This wasn't a big cluster fuck of messed upness. I could handle this. I'd get the prince cured. He'd go home happy and healthy and probably off to fuck one of his ladies at court and forget all about me.

Mother of gods, what was wrong with me?

I grabbed fistfuls of my thick hair and let out a long-frustrated growl.

"Tara."

My eyes jerked up to meet William's gaze. He'd said my name before but never in that gentle, almost loving manner. It made my heart twitter and I told it to shut the fuck up before it got me in anymore trouble.

"What?" I sniffed, swiping at my face, the traitorous tears coming anyway.

William leaned toward me, the hand on his good arm lifting. My skin burned and tingled where his thumb caught the tears sliding down my face. "How could I hate someone so strong, so resilient. Someone with such a mouth on her."

I giggled a little.

"When I walked into your store, I expected to meet some crazy old witch who fed off the misfortune of others...definitely not..." he trailed off his eyes dancing over my face before he cleared his throat and leaned back against the wall.

"Definitely not what?" I prodded, needing to know what he was thinking.

William peered up at me beneath those long lashes. The uncertainty in his eyes mixed with the pain had this perfect kind of vulnerability that made me want to kiss him. "Definitely not...you."

We stared at each other for a long moment, the air in the hole thickening until I pulled at the collar of my dress and cleared my throat. "Well, I can tell you, if you had come a decade earlier you would have run into my grandma." I tucked my hair behind my ear and shifted onto my knees. "She was everything you said and more. I mean…there was that incident with those kids."

The prince didn't speak for a moment. I thought for sure the pain had been too much and he'd passed out. When I looked over at him, he was still staring at me this time with a different kind of heat in his eyes.

"What?" I shifted once more, pulling down the skirt of my dress which was significantly shorter now. "Why do you keep staring at me like that? Is there something on my face?" I touched my cheek, the blood rushing to the surface.

"Not yet." he twisted toward me and then cried out in pain, his hand going to thigh. "Shit. That does not feel good."

"Oh…uh…I should probably check on that one too." I reached for the cut on the leg of his pants. I tried to find a way to look at it without brushing up against the hardness at the front of his pants. Which was proving to be impossible. Every time I pulled on the tear in his pants the side of my hand would brush the edge of it.

William groaned.

I jerked my hands back. "Did that hurt?"

Those pale arctic-colored eyes burned into me. "No."

CHAPTER FIFTEEN

"NO?" I PARROTED BACK to him, not sure I heard him right. "It doesn't hurt or no, it does?" I let my finger graze the side of his cock through his pants once more.

"No," he hissed through his teeth, his hips arching up to meet my touch. "That doesn't hurt in the way that you mean."

"So...I should probably stop." I moved my hand back to the wounded area, fingering the edge of the cut. "This one doesn't look too bad but we should probably get you out of your pants...I mean," I cleared my throat and didn't look him in the eye as I added on, "so I can see it more clearly."

"Right."

The low and husky sound of his voice sent tingles across my skin.

William used the hand on his good arm to untie his pants. I stopped him with mine. Lifting his gaze to mine, he raised his eyebrows in question.

"Let me, you're injured after all."

He inclined his head and placed his hand back on the ground, giving me room to work.

I swallowed thickly while my fingers worked. I didn't know why I was nervous. I'd seen his dick several times now and have even had it pressed up against my most sensitive parts. There was just something so...intimate about being the one to disrobe him. I was the one who was taking his clothes off voluntarily. The one who was using a paper thin excuse to touch him.

"Can you lift your hips?" I asked, my voice coming out in a murmur.

William helped me lift his hips, while I slid his pants down just past the wound. His cock jutted out into the air, bobbing from the momentum of finally being free of its cloth confines.

This close up, it was easy to see the way the candy cane stripes decorated the flesh of his length but didn't take away from the natural shape of him. A long thick vein ran up the underside of his cock, ending at the perfectly shaped mushroom head.

Suddenly, I remembered what he'd said to me at my aunt's house. Four fingers. He said it would take four fingers to be ready for him. He'd been right.

I licked my lips and ached for it. I wanted it in my hand, in my mouth, inside of me. Wherever I could get it, I wanted — no, needed — it right then and there.

Unfortunately, that wasn't going to happen. Not only because of the words the prince had said to me before about not wanting me but also the fact that he was injured. Any type of sexy fun would have to be delicately managed.

Ripping another strip of lace from my skirt, I tried to ignore the hot heat that came from his cock while I looped it around his thigh. My fingers grazed the underside of his length, his balls pressing up against my hand.

To William's credit, he handled it all gentlemanly like. Far more than I expected from him. Most men would have already tried to get me on their dicks at this point but maybe that's another reason to remember that he didn't want me.

I busied myself with making sure the lace was secure over his cut while thinking out loud. "So, if you haven't tried to see if someone kissing you would make it worse… what have you tried?"

I could feel his eyes on me while I worked. It did not make it any easier to ignore the hard and throbbing thing a few inches from my hands.

"No one has brought me to completion with their hands or mouth if that is what you mean."

"What?" I lifted my head, gaping at him. "No one has touched you that way? Out of all the women you fucked to get this far, you haven't gotten off a single time outside of your own hand?"

William shrugged. "If they had then I would not be able to fulfill their needs and I am anything if not a generous ruler." He smirked at this statement and I had half a mind to smack him on the arm for it.

"Yes, I can see you are very giving." I didn't hide the sarcasm in my voice. However, my next question was anything but sarcastic. "You were joking when you said it tasted like a candy cane right?"

He arched a brow.

"Like one of the women has tried to taste it? You can't just look at a dick like that and think 'oh I need that inside me' without also thinking about what you taste like too?" He stared at me until my face heated.

"Have you?"

I pretended to tie the knots of his wound. "Have I what?"

"Thought about it," he purred, reaching a hand out and wrapping it around the base of his cock. He teased it up his length, squeezing every so often and letting out a groan that would be forever implanted into my mind.

My mouth hung open. I couldn't pull my eyes away from the hand on his cock. It stroked up and down in a quickening pace, thick liquid glistened at the opening on the tip.

"Tara," the prince said my name in a way that I had only heard in my head when my own fingers were deep inside of me. "Taste it. You know you want to."

I clipped my mouth shut and shook my head. "I can't. You're hurt. I don't want to make it worse."

William grabbed my chin and pressed his mouth to mine.

I gasped into his mouth, startled by the action. His tongue entered swiftly, tangling with mine and searching out every crevice of my mouth. I moaned into the kiss, letting myself sink into it just a bit before pulling back.

"No... we can't... you'll get worse."

He laced one of my hands with his and wrapped it around his cock, making me squeeze it tightly. "Help me forget how much this hurts. I did, after all, get injured for you."

I gave him a flat look. "You're really going to play that card so I'll suck your dick."

His fingers tangled in the curls of my hair. "You don't have to suck it, just touch it. We both know you want to. If not for one reason..." he trailed off his eyes dipping to the space between my thighs. "Then to satisfy that curiosity of yours."

The way he looked at me almost dared me to do it. Like he didn't think that I would.

I could walk away right there. Leave him aching and wanting for more. I could not cross that line. Though, if someone else knew what had already transpired between us, they would say that we'd already well and truly skipped over the line and this wouldn't make much of a difference in any case.

However, I was never one to back down from a challenge. I was however the type to make it worthwhile for me.

Gripping his cock in my hand, I tested out how far my fingers went around him. A pretty good gap kept them from touching and I wondered out loud, "Is your size an added effect from the curse or have you always been this endowed?"

William pressed his lips tightly together, his gaze fixed on my face.

I released his dick. "If we're doing this for my curiosity then you have to answer the questions or I'm going to stop."

"Always," William bit out.

I hummed, replacing my hand and lightly sliding it up and down his length. "It seems that the integrity of your cock is still the same, though, a bit sticky." I frowned and lifted my hand, feeling the stickiness with each fingertip.

Keeping eye contact with William, I brought my hand to my face and sniffed it. "Smells like peppermint." I slid my tongue out and lapped at my hand, before slipping several fingers into my mouth with a long drawn-out hum. I pulled them out with a loud pop. "Definitely tastes like peppermint."

"Oh fuck me," William groaned. "You are getting some kind of sick enjoyment out of this, aren't you?"

"You know," I tapped my chin, ignoring his question completely. "I think that woman is a genius. She really thought about your punishment. Down to the last detail."

William grabbed me by the neck and yanked me close enough until our noses bumped. "If you don't put your mouth on me soon, I'm going to explode everywhere before you even get your questions out."

"Hold onto your cock, Willie. Don't get your candy cane in a twist." I smacked my lips against his and then dipped down and took a long lick of his candy cane dick. "Yep. Just like peppermint."

CHAPTER SIXTEEN

THERE WAS SOMETHING SWEET and salty about the taste of William's dick. There was the main peppermint taste of course but underneath that there was still that masculine taste of him.

I lapped at the tip, sliding my tongue around the top before dipping it into the slit on top. "Definitely got every detail down to the very taste."

"Fuck," the prince cried out, his hand tangled in my hair. "Please, for the love of all that is good, don't stop."

I grinned around his cock, bobbing down further until my mouth was so full that saliva dripped out of my mouth. I swallowed, trying to get him further down.

William pushed my head down further, helping me get past the gag reflex. Even with him down my throat, I still couldn't fit all of him in my mouth. My hand wrapped around the remaining part of him, squeezing and pulling it before alternating to cupping his balls. He hummed at the feeling and I squeezed them until the sound he made was more of a gurgling moan.

Someone liked it rough.

My inner thighs were soaked by now just from having William in my mouth. The sounds he was making, the taste of him, just the feel of him beneath my hand made my clit throb and my pussy ache to be filled.

"Oh, my... fuck. You're so good at that."

I hummed so I vibrated around his cock, and his hips bucked up with a gasp. His thighs tensed underneath my hands and I popped off of him.

William panted and stared at me. "What? What is it?"

Letting my lips slide up into a mischievous grin, I proceeded to wipe the sides of my mouth. "What do you mean? Nothing's wrong."

He growled and tugged on my hair. "Oh, witch. You are playing a dangerous game."

"I don't know what you mean?" I opened my eyes wide and blinked innocently at him. "I'm just trying to get the full scope of your condition. You can't think I can do that if you get off so quickly, can you?"

"Believe me, I won't go down just after one time." He was practically vibrating off the floor, his whole body tensing with the need to release.

I stroked a finger down the side of him. "You know, I don't know. We wouldn't want your condition to get worse. If you come then the curse could crawl further up your torso than it is." I trailed my fingers down his length and up his pelvis where the red and white ended.

"I think that is a risk I am willing to take." He tugged on my hair, a desperate look filling his eyes. "Don't make me beg."

"Oh, I think I would like that." I licked my lips and smiled. "I would like that very much."

William stroked the side of my face, moving his thumb along the line of my lower lip. "You sure like to talk a lot. Maybe you should put that mouth to good use and suck my cock like a good girl."

My mouth fell open, and I made a small squeaking sound that resembled a chipmunk. "Um... yeah, okay. I can do that."

I didn't start slow this time. I pulled his tip into my mouth, hollowing my cheeks out until William made a long, drawn-out groan. His hands tangled in my hair, pushing me further down as he growled out, "Yes, that's it. Take your prince's cock like a good girl."

"Oh, I bet you say that to all the ladies at court."

I almost choked on his cock.

My head whipped up to see my best friend's icy blue bob poking through the hole's entrance.

Mortification filled me.

Jumping up from the ground, I bumped my head on the roof of the cave. "Shit. Fuck. Ow, that hurt."

"Tell me about it," William grunted, turning away from the entrance as he put his dick away.

I rubbed my head, glaring down at him.

"You know, the wolf told me you were taking care of the prince, but he didn't tell me you were taking care of him." She smirked, letting her eyes bounce between the two of us.

"Oh Bianca, shut up." I smacked her on the head and pushed her back through the entrance. "Where's Percy?"

The blue-haired witch moved out of the way so I could crawl out after her. Her blue lashes fluttered as she pinched her pale pink lips. Her skin, which was usually as white as the vanilla ice cream on her mountain, changed to a deep fuchsia.

"He's tied up at the moment," she muttered, brushing imaginary dirt off her violet-colored pants. She crossed her arms over the top of her small chest, making the long billowy sleeves of her light purple tunic bunch up.

The one thing I liked best about my best friend was she didn't follow the regular standards for her kind. Ice witches were all the rage a while before, and everyone had to look like some magical snow queen. Not Bianca. She firmly stood on the hill of wearing what she wanted and she would be damned if she wore a corset to make some humans happy.

"Is that what took you so long?" I scowled. "He could have died while you were playing hide the pickle with Percy."

Bianca snort-laughed. "I think you were doing quite a bit more than that in there with mister take-your-prince's-cock-like-a-good-girl."

I covered my face with my hands, my cheeks burning hot to the touch. "That's not what it looked like..."

"Really, now?" Bianca cocked her hip to the side and eyeballed me. "Cause it looked like he was balls deep in your mouth."

"First off." I waved a finger at her. "He's too big for that. Second off, I was just checking his condition, and he's in a lot of pain. I was doing what any store owner would do when a customer gets hurt on their watch."

Bianca snickered. "I think you went a little above and beyond the terms of service there."

"Can you two argue about this after you get me out of here?" William's voice called out of the cave. "My arm is getting numb and my head feels fuzzy."

"Oh right. Crap." Bianca knelt by the entrance and turned to me. "Do you want to grab him and hand him through, or do you want me to?"

"I'll do it," I snapped, not because I didn't want her to touch him. She could touch him all she wanted. I didn't want the prince to hurt even more if she wasn't careful.

I climbed back through the hole and knelt at William's side. "Sorry about that." I waved my hand back toward Bianca. "She's a little... she's a..." I huffed a laugh. "She's Bianca."

The prince gave me a lazy smile, or maybe it was from the blood loss. "The bitch Percy talked about before?"

"Yeah..." I leaned down and wrapped my arm around his waist. "Look about before..."

"Are you coming or what?" Bianca shouted into the entrance. "I don't like being in this territory after dark. That vampire is a pain in the ass."

I almost told her that Blackthorn shouldn't be a problem anymore. Then realized that he might not be out anymore. I didn't know how long it took vampires to recover. It had been a while and he could be hunting us down right now.

"You're going to have to help me out here," I grunted, my legs and arms straining to lift his weight. "We just have to get you out of here, and then Bianca can help me get you to her place."

William leaned on me, his body pressed up against mine. I tried to focus on the fact that he was in serious pain and not on the fact that his breath was on my neck and his dick poking me in the side of the leg. I was such a horrible, terrible person.

"B," I called through the hole, "a little help here?"

Her pale arms shot through the opening, and I shifted the prince from my arms into hers. I fed him through the hole until his legs and feet were through. Then I crawled out after him and helped Bianca load him into the cart she had stashed behind a tree.

"Well, he certainly looks like a prince..." Bianca commented, her eyes trailing over him before arching a brow at me. "You couldn't have flown to my place? Might have avoided... this." She waved a hand at his injuries.

"Believe me, if you had met him before, you wouldn't want to be anywhere near him for a long period of time."

William grunted and shifted in the cart. "Thanks a lot. If it's all the same to you, I think I'm going to pass out now."

CHAPTER SEVENTEEN

WITH MAGIC PULLING THE cart behind us, Bianca and I walked steadily to her house. I wanted to run but Bianca insisted the cart wouldn't move that fast. We'd have to push it ourselves and that would dismiss the point of running.

So here we were walking... so fucking slow that a snail could outrun us. I glanced back at William, who hadn't woken up since he passed out in the cart. Worry ate at my stomach and I chewed on the inside of my cheek.

"Stop fretting."

I shot her a look. "You would be too if it was your prince — I mean customer — in the cart. He could die and it would be all my fault."

"Oh, honey." Bianca wrapped an arm around my shoulders and pulled me into her side. "You really care about him, don't you?"

"What?" I lifted my head from her shoulder and blinked at her. "No. No. I don't care about him. I... he's a jerk. He sleeps with anything that can walk. I mean seriously, how do you think he got into this problem in the first place?"

"I can see that." Bianca bobbed her head and shot a look over at the prince's prone form. "You know, sometimes we can't help who we fall for."

"What?" I squeaked out. "Who's falling? I'm... I'm not falling."

"Oh, sweetie. It's okay." she pressed her lips to my forehead. "We've all fallen for someone we shouldn't have. No one is judging you. Besides..." she smiled slyly back at the prince. "I don't think anyone could blame you. He is one beautiful man."

"Until he opens his mouth."

She scoffed. "You don't need to talk to fuck. If you don't bang him, I might."

I wrinkled my nose at her. "Aren't you allergic to peppermint?"

Giving me a coy smile, she sighed dramatically. "Oh, but what a way to go."

I snorted. "You say that now but you forget the whole 'his lover cursed his dick' thing. Not exactly the makings of a great partner."

"Yes, there is that," she paused and then frowned deeply. "How exactly did that happen?"

Wrapping my arms around my middle, I leaned against her once more. "I sold one of those make your own curses to a woman — who, by the way, seemed innocent enough. Turns out she was quite a bit more creative than I gave her credit for."

"I would say so..." Bianca giggled, "... at least, she didn't make it rot and fall off. I had a scorned lover once who did that to a man. Not pretty. There was no saving that one."

I grimaced at the imagery. "I couldn't imagine hating someone that much. I mean, the prince is a dick but still he's got his good points. He stood up to Blackthorn for me."

"He did not," Bianca gasped, then shot a look at him. "Is that how he got injured?"

I nodded grimly. "Yeah. Blackthorn could smell him on me and thought the worse. He challenged him to a fight if he didn't relinquish his claim on me."

"And did he?"

"Did he what?" I stared dreamily at the prince, remembering what he did for me.

"Relinquish his claim."

"Uh..." I looked away, the trees becoming increasingly interesting. "No. He didn't."

Bianca was quiet for a few moments and then said, her voice suspiciously calm and pleasant. "Let me get this right. This man came to you to break the curse that you haphazardly sold to one of his lovers. He tried to protect you against Percy — oh yeah, he told me — and he went toe to toe with the most dangerous creature in this forest, almost died, and for no other reason than to help you?"

"Well... when you put it that way," I sighed and let my head hang, my hair covering the sides of my face. "Maybe I'm the one who's a complete asshole."

"Tara," she brushed my hair away from my face. "No, you're not. You just made a mistake. We all do." She looped her arm through mine, pulling me close. "But the important thing is that you are trying to fix it. If you were your grandmother, you'd have bitten his dick off and used it for ganache after you battered and baked his body."

I snort-laughed and shoved her a little on the arm. "Oh, stop it. She would not have. She preferred her food sweet over savory. If anything, she'd have made him into a pie. And maybe a few sweet buns. He does have one fine a—"

"Talking about me?" Percy stepped out from a bundle of trees, an amused look on his face.

"No, we weren't," Bianca snapped, and stalked over to him. "How did you get loose?"

Percy smiled fiendishly. "Don't think that your paltry little ropes can contain the strength of my beast. You're going to have to try harder than that, witch bitch."

Bianca snarled, her eyes glowing a bright blue. "I'll show you, witch bitch."

"Hey, hey," I stepped between the two of them. "You can fight later. I have a prince that needs to be saved. Let's not make it three more bodies to the list."

Bianca settled down, her eyes turning back to normal. "Alright, you're right, you're right. This can wait. The prince is more important." She stalked past Percy with more restraint than I had ever seen her have... until the shifter opened his mouth.

"That's right, you frigid bitch. You couldn't handle me, anyway."

"Oh, now you've done it." Bianca pounced on the shifters, her hands turning to ice while she tried to wrap them around his neck.

I sighed, crossing my arms over my chest as I tapped my foot. "Bunch of children. I swear, they should just fuck each other and get it over with." I let them go at it for a few moments, hoping that would kill some of the tension between them.

It didn't.

Percy shifted and had his jaw wrapped around the middle of Bianca while her ice hands were slowly transforming his upper chest into an icicle.

I stepped up to them and pushed my power at them. "That's enough!" My voice echoed through the forest, making the ground shake and the birds take off in the sky. I wrapped my magic around each of them and ordered, "Let her go, Percy."

He growled and grunted with his mouth full of Bianca.

Rolling my eyes, I tugged the magic rope tighter. "I don't care if she started it. I'm finishing it. Bianca withdraw your magic now. I'm not going to lose William because you two can't get along. Now, behave or I'll lock you in a room until you two fuck it out."

That one phrase did it.

Bianca and Percy stared wide eyed at each other and then detangled themselves quicker than candy coating hardened.

Percy shifted back and stared off to the side, unable to look Bianca in the face. Though, I probably wouldn't either if I was spouting such an enormous erection as he was. Bianca wasn't much better.

She coughed and stared at the ground, mumbling, "Sorry, he just gets under my skin."

"I get it." My body sagged, and I rubbed my face. "I really do. But this isn't the time. We need to get William fixed up before it's too late."

Bianca patted my shoulder and flicked her fingers, pushing the cart to go faster. "As long as he's living, it won't be too late. We'll save him for you."

I didn't correct her this time.

After seeing the way Bianca and Percy went at each other's throats, it made me think more of the way William and I reacted to each other. Maybe I cared more about the prince than I thought. This had started out as just helping him fix his curse. Now, I wanted nothing more than to have him threatening me again.

CHAPTER EIGHTEEN

PERCY HELPED US HAUL the prince into Bianca's house and into the spare bedroom. I covered him up with several blankets, the chill of her house making me shiver.

"Can't you make it any warmer in here?" I sat on the bed beside the prince and rubbed my arms with my hands.

Bianca gave me a look. "You know I can't. If I warm it up, the entire roof could melt and cave in."

I pursed my lips and peered down at William. "I just don't think the cold is good for him."

"Well, let me whip up a blood replenisher, then we can get about sewing up that arm. That should help him a lot." Bianca shot a look at Percy. "Try not to get any fur on the furniture."

"Try not to get any fur on the furniture," Percy mimicked her after she left the room.

"You really should just bang it out," I told him, not bothering to hide my smile.

"Oh, yeah?" Percy smirked at me. "Is that what you're going to do with his highness once he gets better?"

"No," I quipped. "He doesn't like me, for one."

"Seems like he liked you well enough to let you suck his dick," Bianca called out from the living room.

"Thanks for that," I threw back at her. "And letting someone suck your dick does not necessarily mean they like you."

"Well..." Percy trailed off. "It depends on the male I suppose. If I was in the middle of my mating season, I would let even Blackthorn suck my dick, fangs and all."

I winced at the thought.

"Well, he's not you or overcome by mating instincts." I peered down at William's unconscious form. "He's a prince. So even if he did want me — which he has said many times that he didn't — nothing would come of it. I'm a witch. He's a royal. Plus, there's that whole problem where he will fuck anything that walks."

Percy leaned against the windowsill, deep in thought.

How he could stand to touch the icy structure of Bianca's house was beyond me. I usually met her somewhere in the middle because the cold might not bother her, but my nipples were about to cut through my shirt.

"I'm not so sure you have him right," Percy said after a long moment. "If he would fuck anything that walks, then why didn't he try to screw you the first time you met? Or even up until he fought with Blackthorn?"

I didn't mention the fact that the prince had in fact dry humped me at my aunt's house. It hardly counted. He wasn't in his right mind. And that was what I would chalk what happened in the cave up to. He was in pain and needed a distraction. I was... convenient. That was all.

Not having an answer for Percy, I placed my hand on William's. I frowned. "His skin feels hot."

"That's hard to believe." Percy stepped to the bed. "I run hot but even I'm freezing in here."

I leaned over the prince and placed my hand on his forehead. "Bianca, I need something to help cool him down. He's feverish."

"He is?" Bianca hurried into the room and placed a hand on his forehead. A thin layer of ice spread across his temple. "We need to get that potion into him and get his wounds cleaned up. If he has a fever, he could have an infection."

"Get me something to clean up his wounds. I'll work on that while you make the potion." I stripped his pants from his lower half, throwing the blanket over his dick to save him some dignity, cutting the lace with the knife on the bedside table. "This one is worse than it was back at the cave."

The cut on his leg had swollen up and had a yellowish white tinge pushing at the surface of the skin. I checked the one on his arm as well, removing the rest of the lace covering it. To my surprise, it wasn't any worse. In fact, it looked like it was starting to close on its own.

"How is that possbible?" I asked Percy with a raised brow. "Blackthorn ripped into his arm and barely sliced his leg open."

Cocking his head to the side to see the cuts, Percy commented, "If he bit him on the arm, then it would make sense. They have healing agents in their saliva that close the wounds of their victims over."

"That's considerate of them," I muttered, not believing it for one minute.

"Not really. It's a defense mechanism. If everyone walked around with vampire bites, then they'd hunt them down and there go their hunting grounds. It's really about survival."

I shook my head. I understood the reasoning, but my mind didn't want to comprehend it. By all accounts, that arm should be ten times worse now.

"Here," Bianca handed me the bag of her healing supplies. "I have to go watch the potion or it will ferment and then the only thing it will be good for is giving him a quick death."

I dug through the bag and pulled out some cotton cloth. I wet the cloth with the bottle of clear cleaning liquid and then pressed it to his thigh. William groaned in pain at the pressure.

"Sorry." I winced.

Gently, I swiped around the cut, making sure to clean the entire area. A bit of white puss oozed from the sides, and Percy made a gagging sound.

"I'm gonna..." Percy stepped back and pointed at the door. "I'm going to wait outside."

The wolf seemed a bit green in the face and usually I'd tease him about it. A big bad wolf squeamish. In that moment, the only thing that mattered was helping the prince.

Once I finished cleaning the leg wound, I put on a clean bandage and proceeded to the next one.

This one, while healing, still needed stitches or it would heal up with horrible ridges and dips. I cleaned it as well and then dug into the bag for some thread and a needle. When I found it, I made myself focus on the action itself and not the fact that I was sewing up flesh.

This was like any other needlepoint. Loop it in and then out, across and then again. Don't think about the skin squishing under my fingers. Don't think about the blood. It's fine. You're fine. Everything was fine.

I tied off the stitching and wrapped his arm before running from the room.

"Hey, Tara, I've got the potion," Bianca said, as I ran into the living room.

I made a beeline for the sink and expelled everything in my stomach. When I was done, I turned the water on and wiped my mouth and face with it, cleaning the inside of my mouth out before turning to the others.

"You okay?" Bianca exchanged a look with Percy, who sat at the kitchen table next to the living area, looking just as bad as I felt. "Do you need anything?"

I waved her off. "No, I'm good. Did you say the potion was done?" I looked at the bottle in her hand filled with a murky green liquid. "Is that it?"

"Yeah. Here." She handed me the bottle and then another one that had a pinkish tinge. "This will help with the infection."

"Oh, good. Thanks." I swallowed thickly and took a few deep breaths before steeling myself and walking back into the bedroom.

When I stepped through the bedroom door, I was just thinking about how I would get the potions into the prince while he was unconscious. Then I saw the empty bed and almost dropped the potions. I sat the potions on the side table as my eyes quickly searched the room for the prince.

When I didn't see him immediately, my heart quickened at a painful speed. I opened my mouth to scream for the others when a hand clamped around my neck and jerked me back against a familiar chest.

William's voice growled in my ear. "Silence or I will snap your neck, witch."

CHAPTER NINETEEN

I KEPT MY BODY completely still. Less worried about the prince's threat, I didn't want to confuse him more than he already was with the fever heavy in his head.

William's fingers pressed into my throat, the ability to swallow becoming harder by the minute. I licked my lips and cleared my throat, the vibration making the prince tighten his hold. "William... you're awake."

A low growl rumbled from his chest into my back, his grip squeezing me in warning. "Do not address me so informally, witch."

"Tara," Bianca called out from the kitchen, a questioning tone in her voice. "Are you okay in there?"

William gave my neck another squeeze. "Answer her."

"Y... yes. I'm good. Just a little misunderstanding," I croaked out, and then to William, "You should be in bed. You're not well."

"Don't tell me what I am, witch." He spun me around, gripping my arms in either hand until they caged me in his embrace. "You did this to me. You poisoned me." The intensity of his hatred from his eyes burned into me.

I snorted. "Of all the things I did to you, this was not it."

"Liar," he snarled, jerking me forward. His eyes became unfocused and then his hands on my arms loosened. William swayed on his feet.

This time, I grabbed him by the arms right before he collapsed against me. "Why am I always the one saving your ass?" I grunted against his weight, shifting us so that I could hold him better. "Let's get you back to bed."

Once I had William set on the side of the bed, his eyes fluttered open, peering down at me while I lifted his legs up on the bed. "Unhand me, witch. I'm the crown —"

"Prince, yes, yes, we all know." I sighed and covered him back up. "So why don't you be a good little boy and take your medicine? Then you will feel all better and can get back to deflowering all the ladies at court."

Once I had him tucked back in, I picked up the first of the two potions. "Here, take this."

William's gaze dropped as he glared. "I don't want your poison, witch."

I grabbed his jaw, pinching between his cheeks until he opened his mouth enough to shove the potion bottle into his mouth. "That's it. Take your medicine, good boy."

The prince's eyes narrowed, refusing to swallow.

"Oh, that's how you're gonna be, huh?" My lips curled up on the sides in a vicious smile. "I was hoping you would make it harder for me." Crawling up on the bed, I straddled his waist, careful to avoid his candy cane dick. I wrapped my fingers around his throat and sent a bit of magic into it. My magic tickled the sides of his throat until the prince's eyes watered, and then reluctantly he swallowed.

"There you go," I patted him on the cheek, "that wasn't so bad, now was it?"

William grimaced and turned his head away. "Bitch."

I nodded. "Yeah, yeah. Well, tell me something I haven't heard before." I lifted the other bottle between my two fingers, swinging it slightly. "Now... are we going to do this the easy way or the hard way?"

The prince looked out of the corner of his eye at me for a moment before turning his head back, opening his mouth.

I poured the other potion into his mouth and waited for the telltale signs that he swallowed before settling back on my haunches. "Now, if you would just rest. I promise you'll feel better in no time. And maybe, just maybe, you can get home without losing your favorite body part."

William grunted and his eyes drooped closed.

Sliding off of him, I moved over to the seat beside the bed. I busied myself checking his arm wound, which was closing up even faster now that I'd helped it along, and then the cut on his leg. The edges were already fading to a pale pink rather than the angry red from before. I let my fingers trail over where the swelling had gone down.

"The potion works fast."

I glanced up at Bianca, quickly removing my hand and covering him back up. "It does.

I'll have to get some of those for home. Never know when you're going to need them."

"With the way your luck is going, I'll make you an entire batch." Bianca nudged me on the shoulder.

"Yeah," I breathed out, my gaze lingering on William's face. "It does seem like I have all the bad luck lately."

"I wouldn't call it bad luck..." Bianca leaned on my shoulder, her head propped up against mine. "It brought you prince charming."

I scoffed. "Prince charming. Right." I gestured at the lewd tent in the blanket at William's crotch. "And what do you call that? The thing I'm supposed to kiss to break the spell?"

Bianca chuckled, smacking me on the back. "I think you already got that part down. Besides, if you only needed a kiss to break his spell, you wouldn't be here, now would you?"

"You're right." I cupped my face with my hands. "I didn't want to bring it up until we got the prince out of danger, but I need some trigglewood."

Huffing a disbelieving laugh, Bianca pushed off me and walked across the room. "You don't ask for much, do you?"

I shifted in my seat to face her. "I already got the cauldron from my aunt."

"Where?" Bianca's head bobbed from side to side, searching for the cauldron.

I patted my pocket. "Got it right here."

She leaned against the side of the dresser. "You really think that's the way to break his curse?" Bianca jerked her head toward the prince's tented blanket. "Isn't there another way?"

I fiddled with the folds of my ruined skirt. "If there is, I don't know about it. The woman who did the curse..." I bundled my hair up in my hands before letting it go with a floof. "I may have given her too much freedom with the parameters of her curse."

Bianca narrowed her eyes. "What do you mean?"

Crossing one leg over the other, I locked eyes with my best friend. "I gave her a fully flexible curse to use against her unfaithful lover."

Mouth gaping, Bianca jumped to her feet. "How could you do that? Do you know how dangerous that is?" She raised her voice as she stalked up on me. "How can you be so stupid?"

"Would you lower your voice?" I jumped out of my chair, my hands shushing her as I glanced back at William. I grabbed her by the arm and dragged her out of the bedroom.

Ignoring the beast curled up on the ground in front of the fire, I led Bianca to her cauldron. "Look, I made a mistake, okay? She looked harmless enough, and my latest project preoccupied my mind. I may have been a little loose with my curse giving, now I'm trying to make it right. So can I have the trigglewood or not?"

Bianca shot a look at Percy, who lifted his head from where he was curled up before answering me, "I don't have any."

I blinked. "What do you mean, you don't have any? You're the only supplier in the whole candy forest. How can you, of all people, not have any?"

Rubbing the back of her neck, Bianca avoided my gaze. "Look, I had a big spell that I couldn't get just right and I may have used all of my trigglewood."

"All of it?" I shook my head at her. "How is that even possible? What kind of spell would need that much trigglewood? Talk about doing something dangerous." I stepped toward my friend, placing my hand on her arm. "Are you in some kind of trouble? You can tell me."

The ice witch kept silent for a moment before brushing my hand off. "No. I'm fine. Let's deal with your problem first. Then we can talk about mine." Percy made a huffing sound like a laugh, which earned him a glare from Bianca. "Anyway, I know where I can get some more, but it will take a few days to get there and back."

"Alright, let's go." I started for the door. A pained moan stopped me. William. "Wait. I can't. Someone needs to be here with the prince and..."

Bianca placed a hand on my shoulder. "It's alright. I can do it. You stay here with your prince."

I didn't bother to correct her this time. Part of me did think of him as mine, even if it would never be true.

CHAPTER TWENTY

WATCHING BIANCA WALK AWAY to brave the danger for me was one of the hardest things I'd ever done. I hated the helpless feeling it gave me deep in my gut.

I worried my thumb, my leg bouncing up and down while I stared out the window of the bedroom. Bianca assured me she would be fine. I mean, she had Percy with her, there wasn't anything much scarier than him.

"You really shouldn't bite your nails."

I jolted.

Turning to the bedridden prince, I dropped my hand into my lap. "You're awake..." I moved to get up, then stopped, eyeballing him. "Wait... who am I?"

William peered at me for a moment, confusion in his eyes. "Tara?"

My shoulders relaxed. "No feelings of wanting to break my neck?"

The prince's lips twitched. "Not at the current moment, but if you don't stop looking at me like I'm an invalid, then I could see it coming back..."

"Nothing unusual about that," I giggled and stepped to the bed. I lifted the blanket off of him and checked under the bandage on his arm. "You're going to have quite a scar... I hope that won't deter your bedmate prospects."

"Yes, well," William shifted his arm to look at the stitches. "I don't think I'll be so flexible with my choices from now on. There's something about this whole experience that has put me off ladies at court. They are just too competitive and... sensitive."

I replaced the bandage and sat back, not wanting to let the hope rise inside my chest. "Oh, is that so? Well, if you give up the ladies at court, your choices are going to be a bit limited unless you're planning on finding your comfort in the men at court instead." I shifted my hands down to the waist of his pants. "I'm just going to check the cut on your leg."

Tension filled the room while I lifted the sheet off of him and William arched his hips up off the bed to help me pull his pants down. I tried to avoid looking at his cock when it sprung from his pants, but it was as easy as not looking at a carriage wreck. My eyes stared at the cut on his leg. My mind didn't actually process any of it though. I was far too aware of his eyes on me and his cock just a few inches away.

William's hand grabbed mine, and I froze.

"Oh, did I hurt you?" I lifted my eyes to his face and couldn't breathe. The heat in his gaze had my heart ricocheting into my throat.

"No," the prince said, his voice becoming low and husky like back in the cave. "I was just thinking that we never finished what we started and I am still in some pain. Maybe we could..."

My insides were jumping up and down, wanting nothing more to strip down and ride him until dawn. The rational part of my body not pumped full of hormones said this wasn't a good idea.

He was the prince. Nothing could come of this.

Besides, it was clear from the curse on him he didn't know how to be in a relationship. This would just be sex to him. Crazy, wild, and deliciously hot sex that would ruin me for all other men in the future.

So why exactly was I saying no?

Licking my lips, I cleared my throat and shifted my hand away. "I'm not sure that's a good idea. You're barely recovered, and I don't want to make you worse. I'm surprised your father hasn't sent a search party for you already."

William grabbed my wrist and pulled me down to him. I caught myself with my other hand on the other side of him, so I was leaning on him but not pressing my weight down too much. "I don't give a fuck what my father is thinking right now. Besides, I can't go anywhere until you break my curse."

My eyes flicked to his lips and then back to his eyes. "It is going to take Bianca a few days to get the supplies we need. We could..." I stopped myself, shaking my head and pulling away. "No. We can't. I can't. I have to..."

This time, William let me go.

I hurried from the room, not looking back for fear that I would lose my resolve and jump him.

My skin felt hot and sticky even in the cold air of Bianca's house. Unable to handle my dirty and torn dress any more, I hustled into Bianca's bedroom. Digging into her closet, I found a dress and threw it on her bed.

The form fitting dress would give me far more cleavage than on Bianca. I told myself I wasn't picking this dress for William. It was the only dress Bianca owned. It had nothing to do with him.

Dragging my dress off, I tossed it in the corner. I should just burn the thing. I'd already ruined it.

My feet shuffling against the freezing floor, I went into the bathroom. Turning on the faucet, I sat on the edge while I waited for the water to heat in the porcelain tub. At least Bianca had hot water. I didn't know how anyone could live in such a cold home without having warm baths all the time.

When the tub filled, I pulled my hair up onto the top of my head and slipped beneath the hot surface.

How did I end up in this position?

I poured water over my face and groaned into my hands.

A witch falling for a prince? Nowhere in the fairy tales was that something that would actually happen. What did I expect to happen? We'd have explosively hot sex and it would suddenly solve all the issues that would come from us being together? That's assuming William even wanted to be with me and not just to sleep with me. Experience has shown that was not likely.

I sank up to my neck in the water and sighed, letting the heat wash away the tension of the last few days.

Maybe I should just do it. Get him out of my system. Then maybe I could forget about him when all this was over?

My mind wandered to the way he had looked at me before. That hunger in his gaze made the blue in his eyes darken like the sky before a storm. My body tingled and tightened all over. Heat pooled between my legs, and I rubbed my thighs against one another, trying to ease the ache.

Oh gods, the feel of his hand wrapped around my throat, his cock pressing against my ass. The only thing that would have been better was if he'd bent me over the side of the bed and railed into me right then and there.

My fingers inched between my legs. Thighs falling open, I circled my clit before sliding my fingers between my folds, dipping into my wetness. I brought them back up to the top, moving in slow, torturous circles as my mind wandered.

It settled on the image of him pumping his own cock at the river. His hand moving up and down his long thick shaft, the way he stared at me the whole time while he did it. It was almost enough to make me come.

A crash and yelp of pain jerked me out of my fantasies.

I sat up in the tub, my head tilting to the side, listening for the sound. Another grunt of pain had me climbing out of the tub and grabbing Bianca's robe.

My feet carried me back to the guest room, leaving a trail of water behind me. I found William on the floor, his pants around his ankles and half laying off the bed.

"What in the world are you doing?" I rushed over to the side of the bed, grabbing for the prince. "Did you forget you're injured? You can't just get up on your own."

The prince grabbed a hold of my arm and lifted himself up. I got him back up on the bed and covered up.

Then he looked up. His eyes went wide and then darkened just like in my mind a few moments ago when I was touching myself.

"Um... your... I can see your..." he wet his lips and then looked away, his jaw tightening.

My brow furrowed, and I glanced around. "You can see my what?" Then I glanced down and saw that my wet skin had plastered the white silk robe on me, making my nipples stand out against the fabric. To make matters worse, the middle didn't tie together completely, leaving a long strip of skin showing from my collarbone to my navel.

I grabbed the sides of them and pulled it closed, covering my nipples with my arms. "Did you need something?"

There was a long pause and then William said the one word that broke all my resolve. "You."

CHAPTER TWENTY ONE

I SWALLOWED HARD AGAINST the visceral reaction my body had to William's response. "I'm sorry, what?"

William pinched my chin between his thumb and forefinger. "You heard me. I want you."

Licking my lips, I wrapped my fingers around his hand, inching closer to him. "I don't think that's a good idea. You're not —"

"I don't care." He cupped the back of my neck and jerked me toward him. "There's nothing that would stop me from having you right now."

I opened my mouth to say something sarcastic. William didn't give me the chance. He crashed his lips against mine. Our teeth knocked against each other. His tongue swept across my teeth, demanding entry. I eagerly gave it.

His tongue delved into my mouth, sweeping it and taking over like he was a dying man. My fingers grabbed for his shirt, only to come in contact with his skin. I'd forgotten I'd taken it off before and my fingers slid along the hot, hard planes of his skin. A strangled moan came from me and I surged forward, needing to be closer to him.

William opened his thighs to accommodate me. His cock poked me in the chest and I jerked back a bit.

William grabbed me around my waist and tried to lift me into his lap. He barely lifted me off the floor before he made a pained sound and lowered me back down.

Panting, I smirked. "See, you're not well enough for this."

"Fuck all, I am." William growled, leaning forward to grab my ass. He used his body weight to bring us back up on the bed. I threw one leg on either side of him and whimpered. His cock pressed between us, sliding against my bare core.

Pressing my mouth back against his, I rocked my hips forward so his length rubbed against just the right spot.

Fingers digging into my butt, William grabbed a handful of each cheek and helped me move against him. I'd already prepped my body from my time in the bathtub. So it didn't take more than a few minutes for me to fall apart, crying out into his mouth.

I wanted more.

Untying the robe the rest of the way, William helped me slide it down my arms to pool on the ground. I sat bare in his lap. My body barely registered the cold of the room from the scorching heat coming from William's eyes.

William traced each of my nipples, plucking at them until it was just this side of too much before cupping them in each hand. His mouth lowered as he engulfed one nipple with his mouth, his tongue circling it before pulling it between his teeth. I grabbed the back of his head, pressing him into it, my hips thrusting in several desperate jerks.

My hands pulled at his hair and then found their way to his shoulders. I let my fingers explore his shoulders, enjoying the feel of his muscles beneath my fingers. I searched out his nipples and tweaked them. William's hips jerked against me and then William pivoted us and I was falling.

The mattress met my back, and William hovered over me. His mouth crawled down my body, leaving burning wet kissing in its wake. I reached for his head once more and he pulled away. "Hands above your head."

I narrowed my eyes at him, frowning.

William paused and locked eyes with me. "Put your hands above your head or I'll stop."

Slowly, keeping my eyes locked with his, I lifted my hands above my head. I wasn't against a little play in the bedroom. In fact, I encouraged it. With the prince, I didn't trust him enough to let him take control of me entirely. Which only made the whole situation so much more delicious.

The prince pushed at my knees, spreading my legs wider until I was completely vulnerable to his gaze. William took a moment to just look at me. His thumb brushed against my outer lips, spreading them wide. When he dipped his head down, I held my breath until he stroked a long lick up my core.

My hips arched with each lap of his tongue, trying to get him to settle in on the place I wanted him the most. William pushed my hips back down, shooting me a warning look before letting his tongue trace over my clit.

A high pitched strangled sound ripped out of me.

I lifted my hands to grab him but remembered at the last minute what he'd ordered. Instead, I gripped the sheets in my hands, tightening them into fists as he laved at my clit. He blew on it, his breath cool against my heated skin and my eyes rolled up into my head, my mouth opening in a silent scream.

William dipped his tongue inside of me, drawing out my orgasm and savoring every inch of me.

Breathing slowly, I shifted my hands down and paused. Licking my lips, I whimpered, "Can I touch you?"

His head lifted from between my legs, my orgasm glistening on his chin and lips. "Is that any way to address your prince?"

For a moment, my inner bitch rebelled against the order. I shoved her down with a cooing reminder. If we play his games, we can orgasm more. We desperately wanted that.

In my best sultry voice, I begged, "Please, your highness, can I touch you?"

William moved up to hover over me. "Since you begged so nicely, I suppose I can allow it." His cock bumped against my sensitive core through his pants. That wouldn't do.

Grabbing the top of his pants, I pushed it down until his candy cane coated length popped out. Using my feet, I shoved his pants down his legs.

William chuckled and shifted his legs to get the pants completely off.

Now, with both of us naked, time slowed.

I let my hands slide down his shoulders and down his back, savoring every inch of his body. My fingers found his plump ass and I couldn't help but give it a squeeze.

By the gods, this man was gorgeous.

In any other instance, I would have gotten under him the first moment he stepped into my shop. I probably could have had him too if he hadn't already been so irate about the curse. A part of me wanted to keep him here with me, in this instance, forever. I knew that once we went out that door; we went back to the real world, where he was the prince and I was the outcast witch.

We could never be together. It just couldn't happen.

But this, this could happen.

"You're frowning. What are you thinking about?" William brushed his knuckles across my cheek.

I forced a come hither look onto my face and gave his ass another squeeze. "Just about how much time you must put into your body. Seriously, what do you do at the palace? Just fuck and train, cause this," I gestured at his chiseled physique, "is ridiculous."

William arched his brow. "Do you really want to discuss my job now?" He bumped the tip of his cock against my sex.

I pressed my lips together tightly to hold back the whimper. "I was just thinking..."

"Enough thinking." William grabbed his cock between us, rubbing his tip up and down my folds before circling around my still sensitive clit. "If I'm not inside of your filthy cunt soon, I'm going to explode."

This time when he called me filthy, heat swept over my skin, settling into my core and I wanted nothing more than to have that candy cane dick deep inside of me.

Consequences be damned. Whatever happened after this would happen. At least, I would have the experience of having my prince... at least this once.

CHAPTER TWENTY TWO

MY HAND REACHED BETWEEN us and grasped his cock over his hand. I adjusted it so he pointed at my entrance, our eyes locking together as we slid him in.

William wrapped one of my thighs over his hips as he thrust all the way in. My eyes closed, my mouth falling open in a gasp. The prince hadn't been lying about needing four fingers. He stretched me and filled me like no one had before.

He paused and peered down at me. "Are you alright?"

I shifted, adjusting to his size. Blinking up at him, I swallowed and nodded. "Yes, yes. I'm good. Better than good. No wonder you have so many court ladies willing to sleep with you." I chuckled.

William withdrew and thrust back in. I let out a gasping moan. Not laughing anymore.

"Don't talk about others while I'm inside of you," the prince growled, thrusting until I couldn't remember what I was talking about. "I am the only one you will be thinking about. Who am I?"

Barely able to think straight, I grabbed onto his shoulders, holding on for dear life.

When I didn't respond right away, he wrapped his hand around my throat, giving it a warning squeeze. "Who am I, witch?"

Refusing to let him have all the control, I lifted up and grabbed a handful of his hair, jerking it back until his neck craned. "You're mine and that's all that fucking matters. Now fuck me before I cut your candy cane dick off and make it my own personal toy."

Without warning, William used his good arm to flip me around in his arms, his hand tightening around my throat as he thrust into me from behind. "You want me to fuck you, then shut up and take it like the filthy witch you are."

This time I kept my lips firmly closed. That was until William thrust into me so hard that he hit somewhere deep inside me that had me screaming with just this side of it being too much. My hands searched for something to grab on to so I dug my fingers into his hair again, this time pulling him closer to me as I cried out.

"That's it, take it, witch." his hand slid down my throat until it gripped my breast into a tight squeeze. My inside clenched wildly at the sudden pleasure shooting down to my core. "I'm going to destroy this pussy. It's mine now. No one else will be able to fill you the way I do, you know that?"

I didn't know if that was a rhetorical question or not. Though, I didn't get the chance to answer. William pinched my clit between his fingers and my eyes rolled up as I screamed until my throat hurt.

Heat filled my insides as William came with a growling roar. He pumped inside me a few more times before finally stilling. We collapsed together on the bed, each of us breathing heavily.

"So, that was..." I breathed out, heaving air into my lungs. I rotated my wrist as I tried to catch my breath and finish before just laughing and giving up.

William kissed my shoulder and then laid his chin on it, his facial hair scratching my skin. "Yeah. I know. It really was."

I swallowed and licked my lips. "I think I get why she cursed you."

William chuckled and it vibrated down my spine and inside of me. I groaned and ground my hips back against him. "Oh, don't do that."

"Too much for you?" William stroked down my arm and then along my stomach.

"Never." I angled my head to the side to look at him. "How are you feeling?"

Rotating his shoulder, William grimaced. "A bit sore but it was worth it." He squeezed me closer to him, his fingers tickling along the skin of my hip bone.

"Really?" Shifting around until I faced him, a part of me grew disappointed about no longer having him inside of me. "I wouldn't want you to be in pain because of me."

William leaned his forehead against mine. "I've already been torn into by a vampire for you, what's a little pain when I get to be inside of you."

My heart swelled at his words and it took everything in me not to tell him how I felt. Instead, I kissed him.

This kiss wasn't the savage fight for dominance the others had been. Our lips pressed together, sliding against each other tasting and touching until we were both panting for more.

William withdrew first, his eyes a stormy blue as murmured my name.

"Yes, your highness?" I brushed our noses together.

He wet his lips, the movement brushing his tongue against mine. "I... I think that... I..."

I smiled at him. "The crown prince is at a loss for words? How will our kingdom go on?" I brushed a few stray curls behind his ear and kissed him again.

William's eyes narrowed. "Don't talk to your prince that way."

"Or what?" My grin widening, I flicked my tongue out and licked the tip of his nose. "You'll punish me?"

William flipped me over with a growl, making me squeal. He pressed my face into the mattress and pulled my hips up in the air. "I think you want me to punish you."

I wiggled my ass and scoffed. "You couldn't punish me if you wanted to. You don't have the balls to do it."

A stinging slap hit one side of my ass.

"Is it funny now?" William growled, his hand coming down on the other side.

I jerked, shifting my hips away from him.

"Oh no, you don't." He jerked my hips back to him, his cock bumping against my entrance. "You started this. I'm going to finish it."

"You couldn't finish this just like you couldn't finish Blackthorn." I let out a mocking laugh that turned into a moan as he thrust into me.

"Blackthorn," William snapped out with a grunt, "is a vampire." He placed a hand on my lower back and pushed slightly so that I spread my legs more, making him fit tighter inside of me.

"What's your point?" I shoved my hips back to meet his thrust. "Fuck. Gods. Fuck. Don't stop."

"This is my point." William reached underneath and pressed his thumb against my clit, rotating it a few times.

My whole body shuddered and my legs shook. My heartbeat hard in my chest and white exploded before my eyes until I screamed into the mattress and collapsed in a puddle of sticky goo.

"Now, that's how you finish it," William announced, while I relearned how to breathe.

I said something incoherent, that even I didn't understand.

William chuckled and pulled out of me. I gasped and clutched the covers as I quivered once more.

"We should get you cleaned up." William patted my ass and shifted off the bed. He came back a few moments later with a warm cloth pressed against my dripping core. "You're going to want to clean more thoroughly later, I'm not exactly sure about the repercussions of fucking a candy cane dick."

I made small whimpering sounds, unable to even make a sarcastic remark about his candy cane dick.

"Are you alive in there?" William chuckled with male satisfaction. "Do I need to give you mouth to mouth?"

I waved a hand over with another grunt, barely lifting it off the mattress.

"Alright, then." William rubbed my back and kissed my spine. "I'll see if I can find us something to eat."

The mattress shifted and his footsteps moved away from me. I let my legs drag out until I was laying flat on the bed. I turned my head toward the door to see William standing there with his back to me.

I lifted my head off the mattress, smiling. "I thought you were getting food?"

The prince slowly turned around to face me, his eyes staring down at his completely perfectly normal dick. His eyes locked with mine, disbelief in his voice as he said, "The curse is broken."

CHAPTER TWENTY THREE

IF I THOUGHT WILLIAM'S dick was perfect before seeing it now without the candy coating... gods I wanted to climb all over him again.

William cleared his throat.

Pulling my gaze away from his dick, I met William's amused eyes. "Uh... yeah it looks like..." I cleared my throat and turned my head away, trying to regain some form of self-control. "The curse must have worn off or something."

"You think so?" William crossed the room and climbed back onto the bed.

Turning my head back to him, I forced my eyes to stay on his face. "I guess. I don't know exactly what she said when she gave you the curse so maybe she only meant for it to last a specific amount of time…"

William snorted. "Or you're not as good at curses as you think."

My eyes narrowed and I shoved his chest. "I will have you know my curses are perfectly fine. I haven't had one fail in a long time. So if anything it was your lover that did it." I went to shove him again. William caught my hand and brought it up to his lips, kissing each finger in turn.

"My lover huh? Wouldn't that be you then?" He sucked the tip of my finger into his mouth, his tongue laving at it until my breathing quickened. His cock went from deflated to fully erect in a span of a few seconds.

Damn it. He was not making it easy to focus.

"That would remain to be seen," I commented, my mind going foggy with lust. "We should probably focus on…" I groaned as William's mouth trailed down my hand to the junction of my elbow and then the sensitive skin where my shoulder met my neck.

"We should focus on what?" William purred against my skin, sucking it into his mouth before biting down just enough to know he was going to leave a mark.

Tilting my head to give him better access, I murmured, "We should focus on figuring out how the curse broke... oh gods!" William fingers slid up and down my folds, dipping between them to scoop up my arousal before bringing it to his lips.

My eyes barely open, I watched him licked his fingers clean with a satisfied hum.

"You taste like peppermint," He commented before capturing my lips with his own. "Now, let's see if I can make you taste like the real me."

Before I could protest, William had me flat on my back and my legs thrown up over his shoulders. This time he took his time with me. The tip of him played with my entrance, dipping in and out of it, giving me just enough to make me beg for more.

"Please, William," I gasped, grabbing at his biceps, unable to use my legs to force him all the way inside.

"Please what?" he growled, leaning down to suck one of my nipples into his mouth. He released it with an audible pop, grinning. "Tell me what you want, witch."

Tired of waiting on him to fuck me, I brought my fingers down to my clit, swirling it around while William watched.

He let me touch myself for a few moments, my walls fluttering around his tip before he grabbed my hand and sucked the juices off my fingers. Then he snatched up my other hand and pressed them above my head. "No more touching. I want all your pleasure. All your screams. They're mine. Understood?"

The possessiveness in his tone would have made me fight back usually. Hearing it from William made me quiver with anticipation and desire.

William pinched my nipple at my silence. "Understood?"

"Yes," I moaned, arching into his touch.

He leaned forward and kissed me soundly on the lips. "That's my good girl." Then pushed himself all the way to the hilt.

I gasped. The fullness aching in a good way. My insides fluttered around him, already getting close to the edge. It took everything in me not to take over and take what I wanted from him when I wanted to be his good girl. For him to reward me for doing exactly what he wanted me to do. Then... it would be my turn.

"That's it," William grunted, his grip on my wrists tightening as he thrust in harder. "Tell me how much better I feel without that candy cane bullshit. Tell me you want your prince's cock."

I could barely breathe let alone talk through the intensity of his thrusts. Each one sent me higher and higher until I was just on the edge of that precipice.

When I didn't answer, William released one hand and wrapped it around my throat, his hips stilling.

I cried out, my orgasm pulling away from me.

His grip tightened around my throat until I opened my eyes and glared at him. "For someone who fucks a lot of court ladies you sure need a lot of reassurance."

William leaned down, his length pushing in further making us both moan as he brought his face close to mine. "I don't need to know they want it. They beg for it daily. You on the other hand," he swiveled his hips and I bit back a moan. "Never give me the satisfaction."

My lips curled up into a Cheshire smile. "Why should I?"

Using my magic, I flipped us over before William could retort. Shifting myself into a squatting position, I gathered his wrists together above his head and latched them together with magical rope.

Palming his chest, I leaned down to nip at his lips. "My turn."

The prince's eyes narrowed. "You're going to pay for this, witch."

"Oh," I sank back on his cock, filling myself completely. We both moaned. "Yes, I am. I'm so going to pay." I cupped both breasts, squeezing and pinching my nipples just the way I liked it, my hips rocking back and forth on his cock.

William watched me with storms in his eyes, his jaw clenched tight.

I angled myself forward so my clit and breast rubbed against him with each bob of my hips. This put my face so close to William's I could feel his breath on my face.

"So quiet now, your highness." I panted and closed my eyes briefly, my orgasm building up inside me. "Where's... ah... fuck... where's that commanding mouth now."

William snarled, jerking at the binds on his wrists. "Enjoy it now because when I get loose, I'm going to make you scream for me."

The threat sent me over the edge.

My walls gripped him tight, rolling my hips to draw it out for as long as I could. William watched me the entire time, his eyes never leaving my face. He had far more self-control than I did if he hadn't gotten off after that.

Breathing hard, I sank onto his chest, my face buried in his neck. "You're right," I murmured into his skin, "That was better without the candy cane coating."

William didn't say anything, his jaw flexing against my forehead.

Barely able to lift my head, I flicked my hand and the ropes disappeared.

The prince lowered his arm and then before I could blink I was on my back again, William still hard inside of me with a wicked grin.

"My turn."

CHAPTER TWENTY FOUR

MY WHOLE BODY ACHED in a good way. I lifted my arms over my head, stretching from my fingers to my toes. Gods. I hadn't felt this good in… Well, ever. Maybe Bianca was right. I just needed to bang one out with the prince.

Speaking of, I rolled toward the body heat behind me, slipping my arm over his chest and blinking up at his sleeping face.

Thudum.

I closed my eyes tightly against the growing emotion inside of me.

Fuck. Nope. Bianca was wrong. This wasn't some lust driven emotion.

William and I had sex. So much sex I didn't think my legs would work if I tried to get out of the bed. After I took over, William had made me pay in so many creative ways that I didn't think my body could orgasm again, at least for a week.

I licked my lips and tried to look at him again.

Thudum. Thudump.

Nope.

My heart kept filling with this emotion that made me want to smile and cry all at the same time. I had him with me right now and it was so perfectly perfect that I never wanted this moment to end.

Except...

My eyes drifted to his dick covered by the sheets. The now completely normal dick that had no traces of candy cane coating on it. I checked thoroughly. Which meant that William had no reason to be here anymore. He would have to go back to the palace and resume his duties as the crown prince. And I'd... we'd... fuck.

Squeezing my eyes shut, I shifted on the bed slowly, trying not to wake him. William's arm wrapped around my waist, pulling me closer to him. I sighed, letting myself sink back into his embrace.

I didn't have it that bad. This was just a crush. That was all.

William would go back to his life and I would get my perfect dick shape for my candies and everything would be fine.

I could even look into moving my shop into town. Once I advertised the dick candies as a replica of the prince's, I would get all kinds of customers and I would need a bigger place. I might even have to hire someone to help me. That was the way to go.

Then one day, the prince would see me walking down the street and do a double take. The court lady on his arm would ask him what was wrong, and he'd say that was the one that got away. The one that you will never compare to.

Fucking. Fuck.

Shit. I had to get out of here. I had to get some distance. This wasn't supposed to happen.

Not caring if I woke him now, I slipped out from under his arm and climbed off the bed. William groaned and shifted on the mattress, but didn't wake. I picked up Bianca's robe off the ground and wrapped it around myself, staring down at him once more.

No. This couldn't work. Even if he wanted to, which he had never said so, no one would want me to be a queen and he couldn't give up his throne. I would just have to chalk this up to one of those experiences I could look back on and tell the grandchildren.

A fist clenched around my heart.

Rushing from the room before I fell apart right there on the floor, I made for Bianca's room. My bath water was still in the tub and cold. I emptied the tub and refilled it. Focusing on getting clean, I scrubbed until the scent of the prince came off of me. I didn't need any reminders of him after this day.

I sank under the water, my hair the least of my worries.

Closing my eyes, I let the calm waters around me wash away everything. There was nothing and no one but me and the water. We were perfectly in sync with each other. My world was not crashing apart because of some arrogant, frustrating, wildly handsome, and deliciously perfect prince.

With a growl, I shot up from the water. Breathing heavily, I saw the prince out of the corner of my eye. He leaned against the bathroom door frame, his pants low on his hips and his shirt unbuttoned. It only solidified how completely and utterly screwed I had become.

"I thought you weren't coming back up for a moment there." William held one of Bianca's coffee mugs in his hands, steam coming up from the top of it.

"I thought you were asleep," I commented, avoiding his gaze.

"A few minutes ago, I was. Then someone left me alone in a cold bed and I couldn't sleep anymore." William stepped into the bathroom and knelt by the tub, offering me the cup of coffee. If I wasn't already blindly crazy in love with the man, that gesture right there would have done me in.

I accepted the cup and muttered, "Thanks."

William watched me for a long moment, his fingers tracing the bruises that had formed on my neck. "Did I hurt you?"

I snorted and pulled away from his touch. "Those aren't the first or the last bruises I've gotten from sex."

Out of the corner of my eye, William frowned at me. "Is something wrong?"

Forcing a tight smile on my face, I lifted my gaze to him. "Nope. I'm perfectly fine." I lifted the mug to my mouth, drinking deeply of the liquid to avoid having to talk any further.

The prince studied me for a long moment and then nodded. "Very well. I'm going to find us something to eat. Are you finished with that?"

He retrieved the mug from my hands before I could answer and stalked out of the bathroom.

What had crawled up his butt? I was the one who should be mad. He would get to go back to his life of glamour and fucking everyone with in distance and I would be... alone.

I sucked in a shuddering breath. Yes. Alone. Just how I liked it.

Climbing out of the tub, I wrapped a towel around myself and peeked out of the bathroom. With William nowhere in sight, I stepped into the bedroom. I picked up the dress I'd left out what seemed like a lifetime ago.

I drew the dress over my head, letting it settle on my hips and falling over my legs. Where was Bianca when I needed her? If she was here, then none of this would have happened and I wouldn't feel like this... this... pit of sickness in my stomach.

Since I was placing blame, then I should bring up the fact that if I hadn't sold that curse in the first place, then none of this would have happened. So I only had myself to blame. That was it.

Brushing my hands down the dress, I looked myself over in the mirror. "No more curses. I'm a candy witch only from now on."

"I wouldn't disagree with that."

Swinging around, I stood before William. Somehow, I felt more exposed in the form fitting dress than when I was naked in the bathtub. Maybe it was because of the way the prince was looking at me. Like he equally wanted to ravish me and throttle me.

Well, he could join the club.

Clearing his throat, William lifted his eyes back to my face. "I found some cheese and bread. I admit I don't know how to cook and anything I made would probably be inedible."

A little smile and laugh escaped me, breaking the awkward tension between us.

"Okay, your highness. Let's go see what we can make.' I stepped to the bedroom door with him. "If there's one thing I know how to do, it's cook, and I'll be damned if you don't go home with at least one recipe in your arsenal."

That statement reminded me he was leaving soon, and my stomach rolled. I shoved the feelings down and led him out of the bedroom. "Come on. I'm starving."

CHAPTER TWENTY FIVE

THERE WAS SOMETHING VERY domestic about teaching the prince to cook.

When William had looked at me with those big blue eyes fluttering those long lashes while he told me he couldn't cook, all thoughts of pushing him away went out the window. I blamed it on my need to help people.

That's what I always wanted to do, anyway.

I made a candy store to help people find joy in their life. The expression on their faces when they popped a piece of my candy in their mouths was just... almost better than sex. Okay, maybe not better than sex with William but it was up there.

"So once I crack the egg, what do I do? The prince glanced down into the bowl before him and I laughed.

"You can't put the shells in there unless you want some really crunchy eggs. Here," I took the bowl from him and dumped it out, showing him how to crack the egg without getting any of the shell in the mixture. "Now you try."

I watched him tap the egg on the side of the bowl too softly at first and then too hard, smashing it all over his hands. A smile played on my lips. "Not as easy as it looks, huh?"

William grimaced and shook his hands. "No. It's not. Remind me to give my cooks a raise when we return home."

Home. That one word made me swallow hard.

Pushing down the emotion, I placed my hands on top of his, holding the egg between ours. "See, tap it like so and then there you go. No shell in the mix." I glanced up at him, my hands still holding onto his.

The look of pride on his face made my heart swell. Then those eyes turned down to mine going from pale blue to that stormy gray blue. Another part of me started to wake.

I cleared my throat and stepped back from him, dropping his hands. "Alright, do four more eggs then you need to season it and whisk."

The prince carefully broke four more eggs, taking care not to get any shell in the bowl. I stepped back giving him room to work and myself a chance to breathe.

William had mentioned home. Except he hadn't said anything about going back now that his curse was broken. There wasn't any reason for him to be there anymore. So why hasn't he demanded she take him home?

"Okay, now what?" William turned to me expectantly.

Handing him the salt and pepper, I said, "I don't know what you usually like in your eggs. I know Bianca likes garlic and some spicy pepper flakes but I'm more of a traditionalist."

The price paused and pursed his lips, seeming to think about it. "I'm not sure what the cooks use back home. I'm sure whatever you like will be fine."

"Well then let's add some eye of newt and womblesnaps to it. Give it a little something extra special," I said with all seriousness.

William stared at me wide eyed for a moment and then caught the way my lips fought not to twitch up. "Not funny. I was about to question your tastes. Though, you chose me over the wolf and the vampire so they couldn't be all that bad."

I scoffed and shoved his shoulder. "Who said I chose you? Just because we had sex doesn't mean you won me over."

"Oh?" William leaned against the counter and eyeballed me. "What does one usually have to do to win you over then? Crawl through a bog full of broken glass?"

I leaned into him, lowering my voice to a whisper as my lips brushed his. "For starters." Pulling back before he could deepen the kiss, I pointed at the bowl. "Now hurry up, I'm starving."

William turned back to the bowl, his hands working on the eggs while his eyes kept shifting over to me every few moments. I busied myself making some toast and finding plates, trying not to let the tingly feeling in my stomach make me say something stupid.

Once we sat down to eat, neither of us felt like talking. We sat in companionable silence, the sound of our forks on the plates the only noise in the room. When we were nearly finished, I finally gave in to that nagging part of me that told me to do what was right.

"You know," I picked up our plates and walked to the sink, "now that your curse is broken, you can go home. We don't have to wait for Bianca and Percy to come back."

"Yes, I thought of that." William stayed at the table, his eyes following me around the room.

"Okay," I swallowed down the emotion threatening to pour out of me. "Let me get my things together and we can get going. I'm sure the ladies at court are just beside themselves with worry over their missing prince."

I made it three steps toward the bedroom before William spoke out.

"However..." he began, standing and walking towards me until he stood a foot away. "We're not a hundred percent sure my curse is gone. It could come back right?"

"I suppose so." I chewed on my lower lip, peering up at him beneath my lashes. Hope grew in my chest but I didn't dare to let it encompass me further.

The prince cupped my chin, thumbing my lower lip until I released it from my teeth. "So, it would be prudent to wait until Bianca comes back with the rest of the potion. I wouldn't want to go home and then have to waste all this time coming back again rather than just waiting to get it done now." William stepped closer until our breath mingled. "Don't you agree?"

I licked my lips and bobbed my head. I'd agree to anything he said right then if it meant that he wasn't leaving. Something still nagged at me though.

"What about your father? Won't he worry about you being gone so long?" I pressed myself against his chest, his hands resting on my hips.

William dipped his head down and kissed me once before pulling back to say, "He thinks I'm on a hunting trip."

I pressed my lips against his, nipping at his lips and tongue. I withdrew long enough to ask. "And how long do those usually last?"

"Oh, they are known to last weeks at a time." He slid his hands down to my thighs, lifting me up to wrap my legs around him.

The skirt of my dress bunched up above my thighs pressing my heated core against his stomach.

"Plenty of time then to... ah... figure it all out." I ground myself against him as his mouth found the sensitive part behind my ear, torturing it until I whimpered and bucked with need.

With a growl, William captured my mouth once more, turning us around. I thought he was taking us to the bedroom, then my ass touched the cold kitchen table. William released my lips with a wicked grin before lowering to his knees.

I hadn't put any undergarments on after my bath, leaving my pussy bare to his gaze. I wiggled on the table, impatient to have his mouth and hands on me. William gave me a chastising look.

"Stay still so I can look at you." He brought his mouth close, blowing on my heated flesh until I cried out. "This must be the most magical cunt in all the realm."

I snorted a laugh that turned into a moan at the last second. Panting and groaning between words, I breathed out, "You've sure changed your tune since we first met."

William glanced up at me from between my thighs, the most beautiful sight I'd ever seen. "What can I say? You've won me over. Now, let your prince taste your pleasure."

CHAPTER TWENTY SIX

THE WARM WATER SLOSHED around us as I sat in front of William in the bathtub. He grabbed my hands and tried to keep me from revealing the winning blow.

"You cheat," he cried out when I beat him yet again at Human, Wolf, Vampire. "You must have some psychic abilities, witch." William pressed his lips to the side of my neck and I giggled, leaning into his touch.

"No, you're just a sore loser." I shifted in his arms to look up at him. "You're also easy to read. You are harboring resentment toward Blackthorn and it is clouding your judgment. Making it easy to tell you would always choose wolf or human."

"Maybe I just don't like vampires." He pretended to bite me on the neck and I squealed, trying to climb out of the tub and away from him. "Oh, no you don't, witch. I'm not done with you yet."

He dragged me back into the tub. I scrambled around until we were facing each other. William had both of my wrists caught in his grasp, holding them out to the side.

"Now, this I like. You, naked and wet for me, helpless in my presence." The prince leaned forward and sucked one of my nipples into his mouth.

I cried out and arched my back, shoving more of me into his mouth.

A door slammed somewhere in the house and loud bickering followed.

My eyes popped open and locked with William's before withdrawing myself from his grasp. I climbed out of the tub and found Bianca's robe to wrap around my body. William didn't move from the bath, his eyes on me with bemusement.

"Don't just sit there. You don't want to get caught naked with me do you?" The arguing was growing louder now and my pulse began to pump faster.

William grabbed my hand, bringing my fingers to his lips. "Maybe I don't care if we get caught together. Maybe I want them to know you're mine."

His words caused something in my heart to swell and desire to pool between my thighs once more.

I shook my head, not letting myself get distracted. "Well, I don't like getting caught with my panties down." Withdrawing my hand from his, I tied the robe tighter. "I'm just going to go see what all the yelling is about."

"Whatever you need to tell yourself, love." William chuckled after me.

When I stepped into Bianca's bedroom, I realized I didn't have anything else to wear. William had thoroughly stripped me of my dress and it still laid somewhere in the kitchen. My face heated with mortification just seconds before I heard Bianca say, "What's this doing in here?"

Stealing myself to face her, I breathed in deep and then let it go before opening the bedroom door. "Bianca, Percy. You're back!"

Bianca's head turned toward me, her eyes narrowing on the robe I was wearing. "I see you've made yourself comfortable."

"Very, actually," I grinned at her, knowing she didn't really care if I went through her stuff. "What's all the yelling about?"

Bianca shot a glare at Percy, giving me a chance to look them over. Both of them were a bit worse for wear. Bianca's normally silky smooth hair was a bird's nest of a disaster, while some kind of orangish brown mud covered both of them from head to toe.

"I don't want to talk about it," Bianca stated a moment later, and then tossed me a brown bag. "Here's the trigglewood. You better not use all of it because it was not easy to get."

I held back a laugh at their appearance and nodded. "Of course, sure. I'll be careful with it."

"Where's your prince?" Percy asked at last, his nose sniffing the surrounding air. His eyes widened and then narrowed on me. "It seems someone was having more fun than we were."

I flushed and crossed my arms over my chest. "That's so disturbing. Stop that."

Bianca smirked and cocked her head to the side. "Well? What was it like to be fucked by a candy cane dick?"

Throwing up my hands, I stalked over to her and grabbed the dress from her hands. "You two are insufferable. Thank you for the trigglewood. Now you can kindly fuck off." I pivoted to head back to the bathroom when William appeared in the doorway, his shirt off and his pants hanging loose on his hips.

My mouth watered instantly.

Gods. Why was I so attracted to this man?

"I see your friends have returned." He leaned against the doorframe, eyeing the room with amusement. "Did you get what you were looking for?"

I held up the bag. "Yes. Now let's get going."

"Hold on a second." Bianca frowned, staring blatantly at the prince's crotch. "What's going on with his dick? Why is it not... you know." She made a gesture with her hand. "Pointing out anymore."

"Oh, yeah..." I trailed off, not sure how to explain. "It seems like the curse wore off on its own."

Bianca's brow furrowed.

"Well, that's great." Percy walked toward the prince. "That means you can go home and all this was for nothing." He paused before William. "So, does the kingdom reimburse us for our time and trouble?"

"Since this is supposed to be a secret," William placed his hand on Percy's shoulder. "Not very likely, mutt."

Percy shrugged him off with a laugh. "Well, I had to try. Anyway, I've had enough adventure for one day. I'm out." He waved over his shoulder and made for the door. I chased after him.

"Percy, wait." I grabbed his arm and lowered my voice, my eyes darting over to the others. "Thank you for helping, really. I couldn't have done it without you."

Something sad passed across Percy's eyes before he gave me a lopsided smile. "Of course you could have. I'm nothing but a hindrance to everyone, anyway." He directed his comment at Bianca, who glanced off to the side with a huff. "I'll see you around."

"Be careful," I told him, squeezing his arm one more time before releasing him.

Percy closed the door behind him. I shifted around and arched a brow at Bianca. "So you want to tell me what that was about?"

Bianca shrugged her shoulders. "Not really. Why don't we focus on your problem and then we can deal with mine?"

I shook my head with a laugh. "I wasn't aware you had any problem beyond how to keep this place as cold as possible."

Bianca shot me a rude gesture before turning to her kitchen table with a grimace. "I'm not sure I want to know if you did it on here or not." She waved her hand and a wash rag appeared in it. "I'm just going to have to deep clean my entire house."

Walking into her bedroom, I commented over my shoulder, "Probably for the best."

William tried to follow me into the bedroom, but I held him off. "Just give me a minute, okay? Go see if you can figure out food on your own this time." I offered him a small smile that he didn't quite return, though he did as I asked.

Closing the door behind me, I sank down against the wood of it. There was no denying it now. They were back. There was no more time to drag out the inevitable. No time to pretend like they could ever be anything other than the brief fling that ended way too fast. Then I would never see the prince again.

CHAPTER TWENTY SEVEN

I STAYED IN BIANCA'S bedroom, contemplating what I should do until there was a small knock on the bedroom door.

Terrified and partly hoping it was William coming to check on me, I called out, "Come in."

A pale blue head of hair popped into the bedroom and I blew out the breath I was holding. "Oh, it's just you."

"Well, fuck you too." Bianca smirked, rolling her eyes. She stepped into the room and closed the door behind her with a frown. "So... you want to tell me what the problem is? Why are you hiding out here instead of making the potion? After you just made me run all over the mountain with that mut."

Wrapping my arms around myself, I stared down at the ground and shrugged. "I'm just not feeling up to it right now."

Bianca snorted and sat on the edge of her bed, crossing one long pale leg over the other, bobbing it up and down in place. "You can't lie to me, Tara. I know you better than you know yourself. You're hiding from the prince."

"What?" my voice came out high pitched and I cleared my throat and tried again. "I mean, what? Why would I be hiding from him? He's nothing. He's just a customer complaint that I should have just kicked out the minute he walked into my shop."

Rolling shimmery blue magic around her hand, Bianca nodded slightly. "I get it. He's a pain in the ass. But you also had sex with him. So what's the problem? He's fixed. You'll send him on his way with the cure in case it comes back and everyone is happy..." When I didn't answer right away, she added, "Right?"

I turned my back on her, chewing on my lower lip.

Bianca was right. Of course she was. She was always right. I didn't know what I was worrying about. This was just a little crush.

I'd get over it. I just had to get the prince home and then... and then...

Swallowing down the emotions threatening to overwhelm me, I took a deep breath and turned back around to face her with a small smile. "Yeah. You're right. This is what I wanted. What he wanted. He'll go home and everything will go back to normal."

"Tara." Bianca stood and stepped toward me, her hand out reached.

I brushed past her to the door before she could touch me. I didn't know if I could hold on to myself if she touched me. Instead, I pulled open the bedroom door and called out, "Alright. Let's get this potion made and get you home. There are some court ladies missing their prince."

William glanced up from the book he'd been reading at the window and smiled at me. A genuine smile that filled his entire face.

My breath caught in my chest. I shoved it down deep, telling myself I was just hungry and tired. I wanted to go home. It had nothing to do with those dimples in his cheeks or the heated look he shot my way.

"I think the ladies of the court will have to do without me from now on," William placed the book down and stalked toward me. "I don't think I'll have any time for them anymore."

"Oh? Really?" I arched a brow, not letting him pull me into his arms. Ignoring his frown, I pulled the shrunken cauldron from my pocket and sat it in the middle of the room. I fought to keep my attention on lighting the fire for the cauldron until I felt the heat of him a foot away from me and my shoulders tensed.

William let out a huff and then said, "So, what do we need for this potion? We got the cauldron and the trigglewood. What else?"

Avoiding his gaze, I peered over the contents of Bianca's ingredient shelf. I grabbed a few jars and brought them over to the cauldron. Bianca leaned against the bedroom door frame, watching me with concern in her eyes.

"There are a few things we have to add," I explained to the prince without looking at him. "The trigglewood is the major component to hold everything together. The rest is quite simple. Salt to purify the spirit. Ninroot to wrap it together. Then we need a bit of what the curse entailed." I found my old dress and dug into the pocket and pulled out a small candy cane before coming back and dropping it into the pot.

"Have you had that the whole time?" William asked, his tone that of the prince I'd first met and not the one who had pinned me down and fucked me within an inch of my life.

I slid a sideways glance his way and shrugged. "I grabbed it before we left. Now, if you could spit into the cauldron."

"What?" William gaped at me.

I gestured at the steaming cauldron. "Come on, I can't put in the trigglewood until you add your bit in."

William stepped tentatively forward before spitting into the cauldron's depths. "This has to be the strangest thing I've ever done."

Unable to help myself, I arched a brow at him. "The strangest thing?"

His stormy gaze swept over me, and he licked his lips. I knew he was remembering what I was at that moment. My body grew warm and wet at the memory and his attention on me.

Clearing my throat, I refocused on the potion, stirring it in the cauldron counterclockwise precisely ten times. I'd never learned why it had to be that way or if it was some superstition amongst the witches. Either way, it did the job. The potion came to a boil, the contents a white and red striped mixture.

"Is it supposed to look like that?" William cocked a brow at the thick mixture.

"I don't know. It looks different for each case," I explained, my mind firmly set on the process and not how much closer I was to never seeing the prince again.

Somehow Bianca realized I needed a minute and took over for me. She picked up the bag of trigglewood and ripped the plant's red and white leaves off, dropping them one at a time into the boiling mixture. "Potions and magic aren't as simple as you would think. They are complicated, with many layers, and unique to each individual mixture..." she trailed off before glancing at me. "Just like people."

I ignored her pointed look and busied myself with finding a bottle to contain the mixture. I wanted to get out of here and back home before I did something stupid. Like falling more in love with the arrogant prince.

"I see," William commented, only seeming to half listen to what Bianca said, his eyes boring into my back. "And what exactly will I be doing with this potion?"

Spinning around, I caught the grimace on William's face as he stared at the potion. I fought a smile, approaching the cauldron. Lifting the spoon from its place on the handle, I scooped up the thick liquid, almost the consistency of mud, and spooned it into the bottle. When I was done, I twisted a lid onto it and handed it to the prince.

"Here you go, one candy cane dick cure." I held the bottle out to him, not bothering to hold back my grin as he reluctantly took it from me. His fingers brushed mine, and I jerked my hand back. Luckily, William caught the bottle before it slipped from his fingers, giving me a curious look.

"Well," I turned my eyes away and addressed Bianca, "Thanks for everything. I hate to ask for more, but do you have a spare broom I can borrow?"

"I thought you didn't want to because..." Bianca's eyes drifted over to the prince, or more precisely, his crotch.

"I changed my mind. I'd rather get back sooner than later." Grabbing my things, I bundled up my ruined dress and shoved it into my bag. "Besides, who knows if Blackthorn is waiting for us to come back?"

Bianca brought me a broom, her hand resistant to me when I grabbed it. "Are you sure this is what you want?"

My eyes flicked over to William, who was still staring at the bottle with a nauseated grimace. "Yes, it's better this way. Just like a band aid. Quick and painless."

When I turned to the prince to leave, Bianca's following words trailed after me. "Painless for who?"

CHAPTER TWENTY EIGHT

WHO WOULD HAVE THOUGHT riding back to my house on a broom would be worse than facing the no doubt pissed off vampire? I'd have rather had William's candy cane dick stabbing me in the back than the overbearing tension between us now.

It wasn't exactly easy to ride a broom with a passenger, let alone one who I'd just recently been playing around naked with. Every inch of the prince's front pressed against my back, and it was easy to tell that he was more than happy to be there.

Shifting on the broom, I tried to ignore the throbbing between my thighs that was only getting worse with each brush of the broom against my core.

William growled. "Stop."

"What?" I turned my head toward him. "I didn't hear you."

A hand wrapped around my throat and jerked me back against the prince's chest. "Stop wiggling around or I'm going to bend you over and fuck you right here in the sky."

Trying to ignore the way my body jerked with excitement, I swallowed. "Sorry... maybe we should take a break." I peered down below us, my eyes scanning the area for a good place to land. Finding a hill without a lot of trees in it, I angled the broom to go lower. I kept my attention on the surrounding trees.

I hadn't exaggerated about Blackthorn. He would come back with a vengeance and I didn't want to be here in the forest when he did.

When we landed, William jumped off the broom so fast I could have sworn his ass was on fire.

I picked up the broom and leaned against it, watching as he stalked over to a tree for a moment, muttering to himself, before slamming a fist into the trunk with a snarl.

Huffing a laugh, I tried to break the tension. "What did that tree ever do to you?"

William pivoted on his heel and stared me down.

The intensity of his gaze made me swallow thickly, shifting on my feet. I tucked my hair behind my ear and broke his gaze. "We really shouldn't loiter here. Blackthorn could find us at any moment and —"

"Shut up."

My head snapped up. "What?"

William had crept up on me and stood only a few feet away now. "I said, shut your fucking mouth."

My brows furrowed, and I glared. "You don't get to give me orders, your highness."

His lips twitched. "You didn't seem to have a problem with it before, or was that only when I had my cock inside of you?"

My face flushed. My heart ramping up in my chest, beating so hard that I worried he could hear it. "That was a mistake."

William's brows shot up. "A mistake? So you let me fuck you, take you like a paid whore, let me taste you and come inside of your mouth and now you say that's a mistake?"

Laying out everything that we had done made my body quiver with need. Angry at him and even more so at my body's reaction,

I snarled, baring my teeth at him, "What do you even care? I'm just one of your many conquests. You'll go back to the palace and this will be all over. You go back to sticking your dick into anyone you can, and I'll have what I wanted."

"That's right," the prince grinned viciously at me. "I will go back to the palace and I'll be perfectly happy to find a nice wet noble cunt to fuck and not some filthy witch who's too afraid to admit what she really wants."

"I'm afraid," I scoffed, shoving at his chest. "You're the one who couldn't commit to one woman and got cursed for screwing around. If any of us are afraid, it's you." I shoved him again with a little extra umph from my magic. "I'm the one who just went through all the trouble and danger of finding you a cure when I should have let you just get what you deserved."

William grabbed my wrists, keeping me from shoving him once more. "You think I should be punished?"

I leaned forward until my nose was inches from his own. "I think you should be strapped naked to a pole in the town square so the ladies of the court can use you how you've used them all this time."

"Is that what you think?" William hissed, his grip tightening. "You think those women didn't love every second of it? That they didn't moan and scream the exact same way you did while I did all manner of nasty things to them?"

"I hate you," I spat, wishing I could curse him again just for being so aggravating.

William released my wrists and grabbed me back by the back of the neck. "Good. Then you'll hate me even more after this."

His lips crushed against mine and he had me backed up against a tree in a matter of seconds. Hitching my legs up around his hips, William wasted no time ripping my skirt out of the way so there was nothing between us. When he sank inside of me, we withdrew from the kiss, pulling in air quickly before finding each other's mouths once more.

This wasn't like back at Bianca's. This wasn't a slow teasing love making. We didn't take our time to get to know each other's bodies or wait for the other person to find their pleasure. This time, we battled for dominance. Neither one of us wanting to give in to the other, while we used the other to get what we wanted.

William stabbed into me so hard that I swore the tree he had me up against would have an imprint of it when we were finished. At least, there would be something to come back to so I could remember it really happened and it wasn't just a dream. That for a short time I really had the prince plowing into me like he was a dying man and couldn't live without the feel of my warm flesh surrounding his cock.

My orgasm ripped into me as violently as William fucked me. His mouth released mine and found the side of my neck, sucking and biting me until I knew there was going to be a bruise for days after.

William's body tensed, and he threw back his head with a roar.

I took a moment to catch my breath, William's breath on my throat.

After a moment, he drew away from me. "That was…"

"Never happening again." I shoved him away from me, dropping my legs and straightening the skirt of my dress.

William frowned at me, utter confusion on his face. "Why are you being like this?"

"Like what?" I asked, stepping around him to pick up the broom. "I'm being the same as I always have been. You've known me for what? A span of three days? What makes you think you know me at all?"

The startled look on his face almost made me take it back. I wouldn't though. I had to push him away. He was the prince, and I was just a witch. No one would want me on the throne. There was no way this would never work.

Besides, if his ex cursed him just for cheating on them with another woman, then I couldn't imagine what they would do if they knew he was choosing a witch over them. I'd be lucky if I got shoved into an oven.

It was better for both of us if we just went our separate ways.

"I think I know you pretty well," William stated, coming up behind me. "Being shoved into life-or-death situations every other minute will make you really see the truth about a person."

"And what truth is that?" I swiped a hand over myself, removing the last lingering evidence of him from myself before mounting the broom.

"That you're a good person who would do anything for another person." He grabbed the top of the broomstick. "Someone who will face down monsters to save others and will not stop until they have a solution to a problem. Even if that problem ended up rectifying itself." William gave me a small smile.

I didn't return it.

"Tell me I'm wrong." William brushed his fingertips against my cheek.

I lifted my gaze, seeing the hope in his eyes crushed something inside of me. So I said the only thing that I knew would put an end to this. "I'm just a candy maker keeping an eye on her investment. Fucking you was just checking for quality assurance. Now get on the broom before I leave you here to walk the rest of the way back."

William's expression hardened before he stepped back from me and the broom. "I'd rather walk."

The hardest thing I'd ever done was shrug my shoulders and turn my back on him. "Suit yourself."

CHAPTER TWENTY NINE

I FLEW AWAY FROM the prince. Each foot seemed like a mile. Each second away from him felt like a million. I could barely breathe and hot tracks of tears ran down my face until I finally landed before my house.

There sat my house. Exactly the way I had left it. And William's horse, still in stasis where I put him. I muttered a few words and swept my hand out at the horse. It dropped from its mid stride. It neighed and pranced in place, chittering and throwing its head around.

I sighed and grabbed the reins, talking to her quietly and calmly. "There's a girl. Your owner will be here for you... eventually." I led her over to the house and tied her to the post shaped like a candy cane.

My body froze at the sight of it. Gritting my teeth, I forced myself to look away. He was just a man. Why was I losing my shit over an arrogant son of a bitch? I was better than this.

Sucking in a shuddering breath, I blew it out and straightened. Pushing back my shoulders, I lifted my chin and walked inside.

Only to come face to face with the mess that had gotten me into this situation in the first place. I stepped over the glass and crushed candies, pushing up the shelf that William had knocked over. The sound must have drawn Jax from his hiding place.

"It's a good thing I wasn't a thief," I told the feline, setting my bag on the counter.

Jax licked his paw and rotated his neck. "If you wanted a guard, you should have gotten a dog."

I snorted and put Bianca's broom against the counter before finding my own. Turning back to the mess, I contemplated for a moment just leaving it. Going to my room and curling up in my bed until this aching in my chest went away. Then I rejected that idea as soon as it came to be.

In true witch nature, when something gets you down, you don't lie there and take it. You get up off the ground and hit back harder and faster. Even if it fucking kills you. Better to die standing than to die on your back.

"So..." Jax watched me sweep up the glass and candy. "Where's our... guest?"

Not looking up at him, I answered, "I took care of him."

Dex made a scoffing laugh sound. "That sounds ominous. I hope that doesn't mean that we'll have the whole royal guard down on our heads soon?"

"No," I snapped, brushing the ground a bit harder than needed, ending up throwing half the pile across the room. "Fuck." I threw the broom on the ground and dragged a hand over my face. "Screw this. I'm going to bed."

"It's still light out."

I shot the cat a look before stalking into the back room. There wasn't enough energy or patience in me to deal with cleaning right now. I just needed a moment to breathe. Maybe a bath to get the smell of him off of me.

"Not to point out the obvious..." Jax followed me into the back room, sniffing the air behind me. "But you smell like you've been rolling around in a pool of peppermint cum. Anything you want to share?"

"No."

Jax trailed after me.

I ignored him, turning on the bath and jerking Bianca's dress off of me as fast as possible. I'd offer to wash and return it to her but I'd rather burn it and just buy her a new one.

I sank into the bath, hissing as sensitive parts of me hit the hot water.

Jax hopped up on the edge of the tub, his yellow eyes trailing over my body, lingering on the bruises around my throat and places on my hips. I doubted anyone ever called the prince a gentle lover.

"That looks like it was fun." Jax cocked his head to the side, his ears twitching. "I hope you gave as good as you got."

My face and body flushed at his words. I swiped my face with water and muttered, "Something like that."

"And the prince?"

I leaned back against the tub and blew out a breath. "He's cured."

"And your payment?" Jax licked his fur. "I'm assuming you didn't do all this for nothing?"

"No," I slapped my hand down, water shot up and sprayed Jax. He yowled and jumped off the tub, giving me an aggravated look. "No, I didn't get my payment. No, I don't think I will be getting it. And no, I don't give two fucks about it right now. Just let me take my bath in peace."

"Don't get your tail in a twist. One of us has to be the rational one about all this. This is a business. If you spend all your time fixing the curses you sell, then you won't be able to do anything else then, will you?"

I flicked water at the cat. "Don't you have a mouse to chase or something?"

If the cat could snort, then I was sure he would have. "Let's not pretend you didn't spell this place to be mouse proof. However..." he trailed off, turning on his paws, his tail flicking behind him. "Since apparently I'm not wanted, I will find something else to occupy my time."

When I was finally alone, I breathed out, "Thank you."

Except now that Jax was gone, I was alone with my thoughts. Not something I wanted to be.

Instead of thinking, I focused on washing myself, finding every place the prince had touched, kissed, tasted. I didn't want a single thing left on me that would remind me of him or our time together. The bruises would take longer to get rid of. I'd have to make a poultice to get rid of them faster. I didn't think I could handle waiting weeks for them to disappear by themselves.

By the time I got out of the tub, my fingers and toes were wrinkled and my eyes were sore from crying. I dried off and rubbed lotion all over myself before searching my shelves for some left over healing cream I'd had before.

"Yes." I grabbed the metal container and twisted off the lid. There was barely any of it left. Just enough for me to rub it in one place. I looked in the mirror, my eyes immediately going to the large mark on the side of my neck William had given me just hours ago.

That one. That one had to go.

Scooping the gel substance out, I smoothed it over the bruise, wincing with each touch. Who knew things that felt so good while you were doing them could hurt like a bitch afterward?

I slipped my nightgown over my head and slid under the cool sheets. My head barely hit the pillow when Jax jumped up on the bed. He circled in place before lying down. I closed my eyes and sighed, hoping that for once my mind would listen to me and not make me dream of him.

Before I could drift off to sleep, Jax commented, "The horse is gone."

CHAPTER THIRTY

I SPENT THE NEXT few days cleaning up the shop until it was like the prince was never there. It would have been perfect except the bruises were stubborn and settled on an ugly yellow color even after I made a new batch of healing poultice.

Thankfully, I had plenty to keep my mind off the prince. It took all of my concentration to make each little red candy into the shape of a heart and then even more focus to smash them into little pieces with a hammer.

"I still think you should demand payment," Jax commented from his place on the counter. "You did a service. You should get paid for it."

"Just drop it, Jax." I shot a glare in his direction, dumping the entire tray into the trash. "I'm not asking for it. There is nothing I want from the crown prince anymore."

"Well, that's too bad," Jax mused, licking his paws clean. "Because I think you are going to need him."

My head jerked up from the counter. "What do you mean?"

Jax stared at something behind me. "Because of the guards standing at your front door."

Three large men in red-colored armor stood menacingly at the front door, staring into the shop door window. One of them banged on the door and yelled, "Come out witch, we know you're in there."

My eyes widened.

"Not very bright, are they?" Jax sniffed.

"What do you think they are doing here?" I walked around the counter and took a hesitant step toward the door.

"Well..." Jax meowed, moving closer to me on the counter. "I would assume that it has something to do with the crown prince you want nothing more to do with." He yawned and cocked his head to the side. "Should we go out the back door?"

I pursed my lips at him and inched my way toward the door. "I don't think that would be a good idea. Let's just see what they want."

"Okay," Jax drew out. "I still don't think it's a good idea."

Rolling my eyes at him, I unlocked the front door and opened it. "Hello, gentlemen. How can I help you today?"

The guard who spoke grabbed me by the arms. "You are under arrest for the cursing and kidnapping of the crown prince of Candiopolis."

I blinked at him. "Excuse me?"

"Do not make us get violent, witch. Just come quietly and we will make sure they show you leniency." His words conflicted with the way his fingers bit into my forearms.

"I'm not sure I like your tone," I shot back, pulling against his hold. "And if anyone has anything to complain about, it's me." I leaned my head to the side. "See this? That's from your precious prince. So maybe you should go arrest him!"

"You can take that up with the king." He jerked me out the door and before I had a chance to smack him with my magic, another guard slapped a pair of strange metal cuffs on me with glowing blue marks. "It is useless to resist. We had the court sorcerer make these up for you special."

I tried to push my magic out. I could feel it. It was there. It just couldn't come out. Glaring down at the cuffs, I growled at the guards. "This is ridiculous. I didn't do anything except save your precious prince from a lifetime of embarrassment," then muttered to myself, "And a lot of women, infections."

"Save it for the king." The guard shoved me forward, marching me to a waiting covered cart. "Get in there and be quiet. Or we'll gag you too."

I snorted, rolling my eyes. "Don't threaten me with a good time."

The cart jerked forward, throwing me from my seat and onto the floor. That goddamn prince. I should have listened to Jax and snuck out the back. Or rather, I should have listened to my instincts and turned the prince away in the first place. I wasn't in the business of breaking my curses, only selling them. Which I didn't think I wanted to do that anymore, either.

Unfortunately, it didn't take as long as usual to get to town and even shorter time to the palace once we hit the gates. Then I was being jerked out of the cart and shoved down a set of stone steps.

"You don't have to push," I snapped at the guard roughly moving me. "Where am I going to go in this narrow, dark staircase, to my doom?"

"You could only be so lucky," the guard retorted behind me, but no longer pushed at me to hurry up.

The stairs went round and round until my head spun, and my stomach rolled. Maybe this was my punishment. Maybe they were just going to make me go in circles until I threw up everywhere.

"Here," the guard jerked me to a stop, directing me toward the left and into a damp, cold cell.

The cell was only big enough to hold a cot and a bucket in the corner. They weren't even decent enough to give me a toilet. I jumped as the door clanged shut behind me and the guard jingled the keys in his hands. "Get comfortable. You'll be here for a while."

I spun around and held my chained hands up. "Hold on a minute. Unchain me."

"I don't think so." The guard shook his head. "You'll use your magic to escape, and we can't have that."

Growling, I stomped my foot and grabbed the cell bars as the guard walked away. "This isn't fair. Let me out of here. I want to see the king right now. You hear me? I want to speak to your supervisor!"

When no one came back to let me out, I blew out a breath and sank down on the ground. I grimaced as the damp ground soaked into the bottom of my skirt. Covering my face with my hands, I leaned my head on my knees.

How did I get myself into this situation? How could the prince do this to me? After everything we'd been through together? After what we'd done?

I couldn't believe I ever loved that asshole. This was all some stupid crazy dream and I would wake up from it at any moment.

Closing my eyes, I counted to ten. I opened them and swore. I was still here.

Snarling as I jumped to my feet, I stomped my feet on the ground and smacked my chains on the bars. "Let me out of here, you pompous think-you're-so-great-in-bed, piece of shit!"

"Now, is that anyway to talk about your prince?"

I whipped around so fast that the chain smacked me on the leg. There stood William, looking as delicious as ever, with an amused grin on his face, his clothing replaced with the official maroon jacket with golden buttons undone to show off his muscular chest beneath his white shirt. "You. I should have let you and your candy cane dick rot." Grabbing a hold of the bars of the cell, I clawed at him. "I can't believe you did this to me, you bastard."

"But don't you want your half of the deal?" William cocked his head to the side.

I gnashed my teeth at him. "You and your perfect dick can go jump in the bubble gum swamp."

"Now, that hurts." William pouted for a moment and then surveyed me in the cell. "You know of all the ways I'd dreamed of you. I'd never imagined the cell. Though, the chains..." his smile grew as he stroked his jaw. "Those just do something profound to me."

"Seriously?" I growled, pressing my face against the bars. "You're seriously talking about sex when you had me arrested?"

William shrugged, his hands in his pockets, and sauntered closer to me, just out of reach. "What can I say? I guess I'm just a selfish, vain prince who loves to see filthy witches get what's coming to them."

I scoffed. "You weren't saying that when you were rolling around in this filth."

He flicked my nose and smirked. "Maybe I was just slumming it. Now, if you would excuse me." He adjusted his jacket and stepped back from the cell. "I have some simpering court ladies to deflower. Have a good night."

Then William turned on his boot heel and practically skipped back up the steps all while I yelled every curse I knew in the book at him.

CHAPTER THIRTY ONE

THE BASTARD LEFT ME there overnight. Some obnoxiously silent guard came by at one point and practically tossed a bowl of something that tasted like it used to be mush before someone ate it and threw it back up.

I woke up to the guard clanging on the bars. "Get up, witch. We don't want to keep the king waiting."

Rubbing my neck, I sat up on the smelly cot, grunting as I stretched my aching back. "We wouldn't want that."

The guard snorted. "Funny. Let's go."

At least someone had a sense of humor here. I hoped I could say the same about the king. If he was anything like his son, then he'd yell at me before bending me over the kitchen table.

The guard led me from the cell and up the stairs, not even bothering to hold on to my chains. If I thought he would, I'd have asked for them to be taken off. Unfortunately, it didn't seem like that was going to happen anytime soon.

When we didn't head the way I expected, I frowned. I'd been in the palace one time and that had been to explain to the king that I was, in fact, not like my grandmother and had no desire to eat anyone's children. This was not the way to the throne room.

I poked the guard with my finger. "Where are we going?"

He grunted.

"I'm sorry I don't know that language," I muttered dryly. "You know, if you're going to take me to be tortured, wouldn't it be easier to keep me in the dungeon?"

This time, I got a chuckle from the guard. Not a nice one, but one at least. "If the king planned on torturing you, he wouldn't have fed you."

"You call that food?" I grimaced. "I'm afraid to know what you give to your actual guests."

The guard stopped us before an enormous set of beautiful white and gold embossed double doors. Turning to me, he looked me up and down with an obvious look of distaste. "If I were you, I'd keep that smart mouth to yourself before you do end up on the wrong side of the whipping post."

I saddled up closer to him and murmured seductively, "Again you just keep threatening me with a good time. I'm starting to think maybe you just want me for yourself."

He rolled his eyes and opened the door, shoving me inside. "She's all yours." He closed the door behind me before I could get a chance to catch my bearings.

The room I stood in was a huge step up from the cell I slept in. Two older women stood next to the large four poster bed. Both dressed in plain cotton blue dresses. They took one look at me and then at one another in a way I could only describe as judgmental.

My eyes scanned over the chandelier on the ceiling to the mahogany dresser and fragile knickknacks that I knew Jax would go nuts over before landing back on the two stern faces before me. "So..." I held my wrists out. "Do one of you have the keys to these things?"

"We are under strict orders not to speak to you or try to release you in any way," the first woman stated, stepping toward me. "But since I don't give a flying shit what the prince wants, I'm Philius and this Monique. And unfortunately, neither one of us will be able to release you from your binds. Which of course makes our job more difficult."

"Hello, I'm Tara." I grinned, rocking on my heels. "I think I like you two already."

Philius and Monique spent the next several hours scrubbing me down, plucking, and grooming my hair until I hardly remember sleeping in the dungeon. Then they slipped a pale pink dress over my body that tied at the shoulders. The material was light and airy. I felt like some kind of fairy princess all dolled up for a night of dancing under the moonlight.

"I don't get it." I turned from observing myself in the mirror. "Why put me in the dungeon, only to clean me up and give me this?" I gestured down at myself. "Is this some kind of new torture because I have to say… it's working."

"If they told us these things, we wouldn't be the hired help." Philius adjusted the back of my skirt before ushering me toward the door. "Keep your chin up and you'll come out fine."

The door opened and my grumpy guard waited for me on the other side. He took one look at me, grunted and started to walk away. I looked to Philius for some kind of direction but she had already gone out a side door.

Becoming more confused by the minute, I hurried after the guard until I was trailing just beside him. "So... Do you have a name?"

"Yes."

I smiled at him sweetly. "Do you want to tell me?"

"What would be the point?" The guard stopped us at another set of doors. These ones were much larger and grander than the ones I'd been to before. I knew these ones would lead me into the throne room and to see the king.

My gaze shifted around us, noticing the lack of people loitering around the entryway. I would have expected more nobles to be waiting to see the witch get her punishment. Or at least a line of commoners waiting to plead their cases. The only ones I saw were more servants skittering about as they did their daily chores.

"The point," I continued to the guard with a huff. "Is to get to know you. I don't just go spending so much time with others without at least knowing their names." I waggled my fingers at him with a small smile.

The guard gave a flat look before saying with an air of regret, "Russ."

"Now, was that so hard?" I winked at him and then looped my arm through his. "Well, then Russ, let's get this over with."

Russ knocked on the door, and two other guards opened them from the inside.

Inside the throne room, there were all the people I had expected to be standing outside. They lined the sides of the room, a rope blocking them off from the middle of the room where more guards stood at the ready.

As I walked forward with Russ, they parted to allow me into the center of their circle. At the front of the room sat the king and queen in their thrones, their eyes watching me with a mixture of curiosity and amusement. William was the spitting image of his father, whose features were only softened by those of his mother's.

I searched the room for William and frowned when he was nowhere to be found.

"So, I'm going to be punished for a crime I didn't commit and the asshole couldn't even bother to be here?" I spit out, causing the nobles on the sides of the room to gasp and chatter amongst themselves.

The king and queen simply looked at me and then at each other and chuckled.

When he had composed himself, the king said, smiling, "I can see why our son went to all the trouble to bring you here."

"Yeah, well," I muttered mostly to myself, "I'm just a hoot at parties."

The king cleared his throat and gestured to one of the guards. "Alright, bring them in."

A door to the left side of the room opened and in came William with the blonde woman who cursed him in the first place on his arm, smiling like a cat who ate the gingerbread house. She swept in, large yellow skirts flowing around her and a demur expression. Stopping before the thrones, she curtsied low at the king and queen.

"William," the king began, sitting forward in his seat. "You have brought this woman before us with accusations against," he paused and glanced down at a paper a steward held out to him, "Miss Tara Calliope Grim with the matter in which she bespelled

Lady Daphne into giving you a cursed tea. Is this correct?"

"That is correct, your majesty."

I gaped at them. Were they out of their minds? How could that little conniving wretch think she could pin this on me when I was in this whole mess because of her to begin with? My powers built up inside of me, making me vibrate with the sheer force of it. Unfortunately, the cuffs on my wrists didn't give them anywhere to go, and they just sat there on the edge of blowing everything up.

"And Miss Grim." The king peered down at me. "How do you plead?"

CHAPTER THIRTY TWO

I GLARED AT THE back of the prince's head, contemplating all the ways I wanted to kill him.

The prince who had not once looked at me since the moment he walked into the throne room with that deceitful bitch on his arm. His shoulders stiffened at the force of my stare, his neck muscles visibly tightening.

With a purr in my voice, I released Russ and strolled over to the prince and Daphne. "Why would I, your majesty, wish to harm such a charming prince?" I gave William a pout when he refused to look at me, tiptoeing my fingers up his chest before cupping his chin with my hand. A few of the guards shifted forward, but the king waved them off.

Peering over my shoulder at the king, I commented, "After all, so many ladies of the court here could speak for his charm and virility."

A few of the ladies giggled in the crowd, only to be shushed by their family.

"How dare you touch him?" Daphne screeched at me, her face coming within an inch of mine. "You are lucky to be breathing right now, let alone be in the same room as us. You probably wanted to curse him to get back at them for killing your horrible grandmother."

I released William's face and stepped to Daphne. Who, to my delight, took several steps back from me. "Oh, we're going to play that game, are we? So tell me, Daphne, how exactly did I bespell you into cursing the prince?"

Avoiding my gaze, Daphne spoke to the king and queen. "I went to the witch's shop to buy some of her candy. Many of the townspeople had comments on how much they enjoyed it. Only," she sucked in a breath, blotting at her eyes, "only for her to put some kind of spell on me to... to..." she sniffed and waved a hand at me. "To curse our precious prince."

"Oh my." I placed a hand on my chest and gaped at her. "I did not know you were so invested in the prince because when you showed up at my shop, you wanted to rip his dick off and feed it to a bear."

"That is far more believable," a nearby noble grumbled, earning a laugh from the others.

"Lady Daphne," the king addressed her with a stern look. "Are you sure this woman is responsible for cursing my son? Remember, if you lie to your king, your tongue will be cut out and you will be exiled."

"Oh, please let me be the one to do it," I wiggled my fingers stepping, toward Daphne. "I have so much power building up that I need something to focus it on."

"Hold on there, witch." William grabbed me around the waist and pulled me against his side. "Let's not get ahead of ourselves."

I froze against his front, my body revolting, wetness pooling between my thighs. "Don't touch me."

"Oh?" William brushed my hair behind my ear, his fingers trailing along the side of my neck. "Is this bothering you?"

"Not at all," I said stiffly.

"What?" Daphne gaped at us, her eyes widening to comedic proportions. "Are you two… did you two?"

"What?" I squeaked, shoving away from William. "No, of course not. I just helped him after you cursed his dick into a candy cane."

William stilled as the crowd went silent and then laughter filled the room.

I winced. "I'm guessing no one else knew?"

"No, but they do now," William grumbled, shooting a warning look at the guard next to him, who let out a little chuckle.

"You were supposed to just curse the prince, not cure him. What kind of witch breaks the curse she sold?" Daphne screeched at me, trying to claw at me. The guards grabbed her around the waist, holding her back.

"I didn't break the curse." I shook my head, glancing between her and the prince. "It broke on its own."

"That's impossible." Daphne hissed. "The only way the curse could be broken was if he," pointing an accusing finger at William. "fucked someone he actually cared about."

The court ladies gasped in horror.

"Don't even. You've all had sex with him. You know what he's like." She crossed her arms over her chest and scowled at them.

I exchanged a look with the prince, who only smirked.

"Hold on a moment," the queen interrupted, her finger bobbing between the prince and me. "You said that the only way to break the curse was for my son to have relations with someone he cares about?"

"Obviously, the curse was faulty," Daphne snarled at me.

"The only thing that is faulty is your brain." I stepped toward her once more. William put a hand on my stomach, stopping me from going any further. "My curses are perfect. I didn't even give you any restrictions because I thought you were some poor simpering thing who had been screwed over by him. Not some psychopath."

"William," the queen interrupted again. "Did you and this wi— woman have relations?"

I looked at the queen and then at the prince, my mouth gaping open and closed. "Um... I... we..."

"Yes," William answered, giving me a soft look I'd never seen on his face before. "I did."

"Oh, Richard," the queen grasped her husband's hand. "I do believe our son has finally fallen in love."

"Huh?" I jerked my eyes away from William's and blinked. "I'm sorry. What was that now?"

Before the queen could answer, Daphne cackled. "That's ridiculous. There's no way that he could have possibly fallen in love with her."

I glared at Daphne.

William cupped my chin and turned my face toward him. "Yes, I believe I am in love with this witch."

My lashes fluttered rapidly and I think I forgot how to breathe for a moment until William chuckled and brushed his thumb across my lower lip.

"I never thought I'd make you speechless without sticking something in that pretty mouth of yours," he murmured to me so no one else could hear. Which would have worked had the guard not been right next to us. He cleared his throat and stepped away from us with red cheeks.

"Would you not?" I nudged him with my elbow, shooting a look at everyone around us. "This is not the time or place."

"I can't believe this." Daphne fought against the guards. "I paid you for a curse to make him pay for his promiscuous ways and you end up fucking him yourself? What kind of evil witch are you?"

My eyes slid away from William and settled on her. "The kind that will be more than happy to show you once someone releases me from these." I jerked my cuffed hands at the room.

"I've heard enough," the king waved a hand at the guards holding her. "Take Lady Daphne away. We will deal with her later."

The guards had to drag Daphne kicking and screaming out of the throne room. Once she was gone, everyone turned to me and the prince as if waiting for something magical to happen.

"What are they looking at?" I asked William, getting a bit worried.

"I believe..." William dragged me over to him until our bodies were pressed against one another. "They are waiting for you to tell me you love me too."

"What?" I gaped at him, holding my cuffed hands up against his chest. "How could you even think that? You just had me arrested. Thrown in a disgusting cell overnight, then dressed in this," I fluffed my skirt up with a wrinkle of my nose. "And these!" I held my wrists up to show him the cuffs. "You had me disabled."

William didn't even blink at my words. He waved an old robed man over, who used a small metal stick to unlock my cuffs. "The cuffs were for my guards and my own protection until we could get this resolved."

I rubbed my wrists and grumbled, "I guess I can understand that. I can be a little, curse first, ask questions later."

"As for the cell..." William drew me back to him. "That was for my benefit."

I narrowed my eyes on him. "And what benefit were you getting out of that?"

William stroked his fingers along my collarbone and neck. "Call it payback for leaving me in the woods and removing my mark." His fingers played in the place where he'd bitten me before.

A throat cleared. "Son, I think we are done here. If you would like to take your... witch... somewhere else, more private?"

"No," William retorted, gathering me up in his arms. "I'm not going anywhere until she admits that she loves me, too."

I clucked my tongue. "I'm not sure that I do."

"Maybe you need a reminder," the prince leaned forward, his nose brushing against mine.

"Okay, I think we should all leave now," the king announced. "Court dismissed."

I hardly noticed the people pouring out of the throne room until it was just William and me left.

"I can't love you," I finally explained with a shake of my head. I wanted to pull back from him but couldn't bring myself to remove myself from the warmth of his body. "This wouldn't work."

"Why not?" William brushed his lips against mine. "I love you, you love me. There's nothing standing between us we can't overcome."

My head angled to the side as William's mouth trailed down my neck. "But what about me? I'm a witch. You heard what she said about me. No one is going to want me to be with you let alone, be the queen."

William growled against my throat. "Fuck them. Who cares what they think? I'm the prince. I can marry whoever I want."

"Hold on a second," I pulled away from him. "Who said anything about marriage?"

"Well," William smirked at me. "I thought first we would spend the next few weeks in the bedroom. Then maybe we could work our way through every room in the palace." His fingers skimmed the curve of my breast, brushing against my nipple until it puckered against the fabric.

I swallowed. "Then what?"

"Then..." William's voice lowered, and I leaned myself toward him. "I thought we could spend more time together and then after I spend a lot of time convincing you that no one gives two shits about who I marry, we could, perhaps, be bound together forever."

"Forever is a long time to put up with your shit." William pinched my nipple and I sucked in a breath. "I'm going to need a lot of convincing."

William grabbed me by the back of the neck. "Well then, we better start right now." He crushed his lips to mine.

My fingers curled into his hair, dragging his mouth against mine until I couldn't breathe. William grabbed me by the back of the legs and dropped into his father's throne, my legs on either side of him. His cock pressed against my center, making us both moan.

Pulling my mouth away from his, I ground myself against him and murmured, "Thank the gods for your candy cane dick or we would never have met."

William pulled his cock out of his pants and slipped inside of me. "I think we both know this would have happened eventually. If Daphne hadn't cursed me, someone else would have."

I groaned into his mouth. "If you don't stop talking, I'm going to curse you."

"Best curse ever."

Want to know when Erin's next book comes out?

Be one of the firsts to know when I have a new release, get exclusive sneak peeks, and giveaways. Also, just having fun in general!

Join my Facebook reader group and be part of hive mind!

Titkok more your style follow Erin here:

@erinbedfordauthor

Get three free novellas by joining Erin's newsletter.

ABOUT THE AUTHOR

Erin Bedford is an otaku, recovering coffee addict, and Legend of Zelda fanatic. Her brain is so full of stories that need to be told that she must get them out or explode into a million screaming chibis. Obsessed with fairy tales and bad boys, she hasn't found a story she can't twist to match her deviant mind full of innuendos, snarky humor, and dream guys.

On the outside, she's a work from home mom and bookbinger. One the inside, she's a thirteen-year-old boy screaming to get out and tell you the pervy joke they found online. As an ex-computer programmer, she dreams of one day combining her love for writing and college credits to make the ultimate video game!

Until then, when she's not writing, Erin is devouring as many books as possible on her quest to have the biggest book gut of all time. She's written over thirty books, ranging from paranormal romance, urban fantasy, and even scifi romance.

www.erinbedford.com